GW01086512

OPERATION WARD TEN

OPERATION WARD TEN

AGATHA STRIKES. AGAIN.

Siân Pattenden

* SHORT BOOKS

First published in 2007 by

Short Books

3A Exmouth House

Pine Street

EC1 0JH

10 9 8 7 6 5 4 3 2 1

Copyright ©

Siân Pattenden 2007

Siân Pattenden has asserted her right under the Copyright,
Designs and Patents Act 1988 to be identified as the
author of this work. All rights reserved. No part of this
publication may be reproduced, stored in a retrieval
system or transmitted in any form, or by any means
(electronic, mechanical, or otherwise) without
the prior written permission of both the copyright
owners and the publisher.

A CIP catalogue record for this book
is available from the British Library.

ISBN 978-1-904977-89-6

Printed in the UK by CPI Bookmarque, Croydon, CR0 4TD

CONTENTS

EDITOR'S APOLOGY.

We have been unable to delete all the errors
in the manuscript, particularly the ones
which the ~~brilliant~~ stubborn and often
talentless author was at pains to keep in.
We have now thankfully rectified the
situation but if you see any crossings-out
please ignore them and read the text as it
stands. We are very sorry for any offence
caused. This is not ideal but we hope you,
the reader, will understand.

Freephone
15.2% APR Typical

01202-629-796
TYPICAL **15.2% APR**

The Rottington
A&E department
the hip 'n' happenin' top spot!
it's quite good
is it?
I don't know really.
perhaps not.

BE FREE FROM PEAS

Reprinted courtesy of
The Rottington Herald

PROLOGUE

Everyone says something they don't mean once in a while; everyone does at least one thing in their lifetime that they regret. (Some wear impossibly voluminous trousers for years.) But people learn from their mistakes, once they have recognised them. Even robbers and muggers can eventually see the errors of their ways. ~~Though I doubt it.~~

Agatha Bilke sat in the Accident and Emergency department at the Rottington Hospital and regretted the past few hours. This was not because she had decided to become a decent human being, it was simply that she had become a victim of her own vanity. For all the attention and help she'd received, Agatha was still bad. The Worst Girl Ever Known to Humanity still hated everyone and everything.

Agatha had been caught in a fire – but, incredibly, she had not caused it. She was annoyed with herself. She had endured many months of being told what to do by various people, some of whom were experts in such matters and some who were just nosey parkers. How could she have been so careless as to end up in hospital with burns to her face and arms?

Agatha looked around. Next to her a man was shivering uncontrollably. Another person sitting opposite clutched her head and moaned. Someone in the corner was a bright yellow colour. A&E was not a good place to be.

1. CAULIFLOWER TRINKLE

"*B*rilliant!

The ward was full, but not especially brilliant.

"*Exciting!*"

There were staff and patients milling around, but it wasn't particularly exciting.

"*Glorious!*"

Hmm.

Everyone was aware that a child in the corner bed was shouting. But this did not stop Cauliflower Trinkle. Some observers might suggest that she enjoyed it.

Now there is a very serious problem that some people have and it's called Tourette's syndrome. You may be familiar with it, especially if you're a keen watcher of TV documentaries. Or perhaps you might know someone with

Sometimes in situations of stress
the sufferer might shout out random words

the condition and you are aware of how distressing it is.

Sometimes in situations of stress the sufferer might shout out random words – the first thing that comes into their mind. It may not be polite; it may be *very rude*. The root of the condition is still a mystery to medical science.

Yet, until Miss Trinkle, no one had even dared to suspect that the *inverse* might happen; that she might be in the habit of blurting out complimentary – not offensive – adjectives at any time of the day or night. As someone might swear and look cross, she would exclaim how charming the world was with a big grin on her face. She couldn't help it.

"Have you thought what it would be like to have no ears? *Incredibobble!* We could all wear hats down to our shoulders."

Downstairs in A&E, a nurse wrapped bandages tight around Agatha's head, her long fingernails clipping Agatha's ears. *Silly woman*, she thought. *Can't she see that the skin is tender where it was burned?* Agatha's arms hurt and her cheeks were stinging. She wished she were somewhere else.

How had this happened? It had all started in the park, with a small child and his endless gifts... but the pleasant afternoon had ended abruptly because of Agatha's boundless ambition. She had been stupid, she told herself. Now she could be stuck here for weeks, and she needed to get out, as fast as she could.

2. GIFTS

The toddler handed Agatha a twig.

"Diss Urgharggh!". Next, he fetched a bottle top. He beamed at the girl, and giggled.

Under normal circumstances, a sunny Sunday afternoon in the park was horrible for Agatha. There were people running away from wasps, grown men with no tops on, wet dogs slobbering on dry dogs... But she was rather enjoying this little game. There was a look of sheer joy on the boy's face, bestowing these waste items as if they were pieces of gold. The child's mother – sitting in the nearby café, dolled up and in high heels – was paying no attention to her son at all, preferring to talk to a friend.

Agatha could smell the charred remnants of a disposable barbecue close by – people weren't allowed to bring them to the park but they did so anyway. It made her feel hungry. She wondered whether she should ask the child to get her a sandwich next, but he looked too little to understand. His next offering was an improvement: a lipstick, from his mother's handbag. This was closely followed by a small diary (with nothing written in it), some mascara and a can of hairspray. Agatha started putting the make-up on. (It was probably a bit wobbly – she had no mirror.) This was fun. Perhaps she might be spotted by a passing film director and asked to star in a top movie, with John Cruise in it. She was just thinking about what sort of fight scenes she might be asked to do, and the basic physical fitness regime she would need to start (supervised by a trail-blazing instructor and accompanied by a leading nutritionist), when she was interrupted by the best gift of all: the bag itself.

Now *this* was something. It was made from buttery, soft leather. The tag was marked "Ballencialloise, Paris – Rich Persons Only". It had tassels and locks, buckles and studs. There were perspex sections, a suede pochette for vitamin supplements, four MP3 players (for different moods) and an ornately-embroidered strap. On the front, dead centre, was a diamond in the shape of the Palace of Versailles. Agatha looked over at the owner sitting in the café but she had yet to notice that her belongings had gone.

"Grurghh dat *siiieeeess!*" said the boy.

Bilke decided to keep the bag; she felt no pang of conscience. The woman should have been looking after her son and her property. Ha! But if Agatha was going to carry her new accessory around – for the rest of the day, at least – she would have to look the part. She already had the make-up, now she would get the "big" hair – to look like a Frucci model. She took the hairspray and liberally applied it to her wayward locks.

This was a mistake.

The highly flammable spray flew in a majestic arc over Agatha's (much-examined) head and hit the barbecue behind, which was still smouldering. Giant flames shot up at once, enveloping the notorious problem child.

A moment later, the woman realised her bag had gone and started shouting in a beaky sort of voice: "Thief! Someone has stolen my bag!" And, as if to prove a point: "It's Ballencialloise, you know!"

As a stampede of angry people in even angrier shorts began to hunt for the culprit, the blaze engulfed a bush next to Agatha.

People who had never known fear like it, started to waggle their arms in the air at the sight of the flames, which were growing bigger by the second.

"This is global warming gone mad!"

A teenager took some footage on his mobile phone, in case *Rottington Tonight* needed it later. (NB It was all blurry – you couldn't make out any detail.)

"Oh dear. Oh dear oh dear… WATCH OUT!!!!!!!!!"

The last voice came from the local policeman, Inspector Coddles, who happened to be in a helicopter, trying to land. Today was his special day – the inaugural *Police Matters* presentation by the ponds where he would give a medal to a brave Auntie who had saved her entire family from a hideous (it is true, he wasn't attractive) burglar. Coddles had chosen this particular form of air transport in order to make a spectacular impression. But, as he descended, thick black smoke obscured the ground – he could not see what he was doing. He was about to crash and look quite stupid. Worse still, he might be added to the death toll.

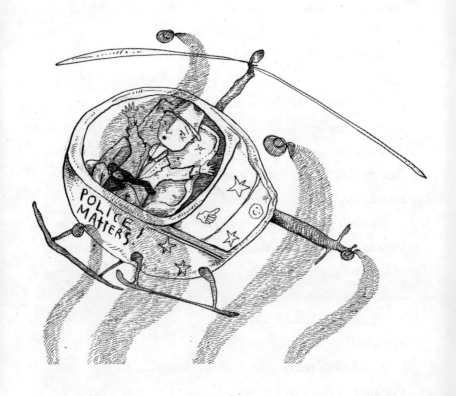

*Crang! Chopperchopper-boooooof! The flying machine
shuddered violently and swung from side to side like a
mosquito might, after too many colas*

3. PHENOMENON

Crang! Crang! Crang!! Chopperchopper-chop! Helicopters are not quiet things. They are full of arrogance and metal, that's why Coddles liked them.

Agatha's situation was worsening. She was sitting in the middle of burning stuff, she was wanted for theft and she was about to be crushed by a helicopter. She also had a very unflattering shade of lipstick on, but that's beside the point.

"A burning bush! Christ is coming! It's one of 'em miracles!"

A crowd of religious people had seized upon the scene, singing *God Rest Ye Merry Gentlemen* in high voices, believing this to be the end of the ~~worm~~ world. A man in sandals was besieged by autograph-hunters, who were convinced that he was the second coming of Jesus (he wasn't so sure.) No one had yet noticed that there was a child in the middle of the phenomenon.

Crang! Chopperchopper-boooooof! The flying machine shuddered violently and swung from side to side like a mosquito might, after too many colas. Coddles, unable to see the ground below, smashed the 'copter into a tree and leapt out of it as fast as he could.

Meanwhile, Agatha had her own escaping to do. She mustered all her strength and, with a swift burst of energy, propelled herself out of the flames.

But she had not quite broken free yet. Agatha suddenly found herself almost face to face with her sworn enemy, Coddles. He was the man who had stopped her fun at the TreadQuietly Clinic and nearly banged her up. Before he had time to recognise her, she started to run. As she did so, she looked down at her arms – they were covered in burns and her face felt hot. Things were not going well.

"Hey hey! Stop!" Someone was shouting at her. Was it Coddles? Or someone after the missing handbag (which was now a pile of ashes)?

Moments later, Agatha fell to the ground, exhausted and aching. "Hey girl!" A member of the religious group had caught up with her. "We've called you an ambulance. You look terrible…"

For the first time, The Worst Girl Ever Known to Humanity had been burnt in a fire. Despite setting numerous buildings aflame, she had always escaped unscathed. This time, when it had been an accident, she had been hurt.

Half an hour later, as Agatha sped off to the Rottington General, a furious Inspector Coddles looked around and had a think. *How had the fire started? And why was it so near the helipad? Things like that didn't happen by chance, you know. It was arson, certainly.* But no one he spoke to knew anything. They were too busy reading passages from Exodus to listen to his law-based questions. This had now gained the status of an official police case, waiting to be solved. Coddles reluctantly wandered over to the Police Matters ceremony on foot.

4. A NEW ARRIVAL...

"*Wonderbra Avenue!*"

Cauliflower walked round to Holbeck's bed.

Holbeck Folbeck didn't stir. He sat constructing a model aeroplane, chewing on a sweet and watching a hand-held DVD player – all at once. Some might argue that he was not behaving like people in hospital normally do – i.e. looking a bit sick and feeling bored – in fact he was sitting in the lap of luxury.

"Can I clean your bedside cabinet?" said Cauliflower.

"No, please don't. I have a woman who comes in at 4.30pm." Holbeck was heir to the great *Folbecks' Mints* fortune.

Then Cauliflower noticed what he was doing.

"You're eating my nuggat!" (By this she meant nougat.)

"You stole it from my bed!"

"I merely borrowed the packet to look at and a piece fell into my mouth."

"*Holbeck!* But it's *mine!* Mine! You've got all the mints in the world and yet you still want to steal other people's property." Cauliflower was nothing if not possessive.

"Oh, get over it, Trinkle," said Holbeck. He wasn't going to get angry. "I just wanted to swap, that's all. When you've eaten as many mints as I have, the thought of another is a little tiresome."

He threw a tube of *Folbecks' Imperials* over to Cauliflower and flicked a switch on the wall, which automatically drew a set of curtains around him.

"As sole patient of the Dorey Wing, I must ask you to leave," said Holbeck as he disappeared from view.

Ah, how lonely Trinkle felt. She longed for a true friend with whom she could become close, someone with whom she could share her enthusiasm – not like Holbeck, who had made it clear that he wanted nothing to do with her.

Holbeck's parents could afford private treatment. His four-poster was placed in a corner of the ward that had been named the Dorey Wing – after local celebrity Paul who officially opened it last year. There were flowers by his bedside at all times, and a rich carpet, which seemed to

*Some might argue that Holbeck was not
behaving like people in hospital normally do*

attract biscuit crumbs more than repel them. He wore a silk dressing gown and sometimes a monocle if he was reading a magazine. His luxurious duvet cover had pictures of mean livin' rap stars on it. In every other respect, Holbeck Folbeck received the same treatment from the team of dedicated medical professionals as the rest of the ward. But Holbeck *felt* privileged and that was the point. He was pleased to have been given such advantages early on in life and thrived on it.

The problem with the ward was that all the children had been there too long. They had grown complacent. Holbeck had something wrong with his foot, but no X-ray had located a sprain or fracture. Fellow patient Dennis Guffe claimed to have dreadful stomach pains, but no doctor had ever found the cause. Lynda Peanuts was attached – literally and emotionally – to a drip but didn't physically need one. Cauliflower may have been the only one who actually had a real medical condition. Not that it gained her much sympathy.

Inevitably, the children became rather set in their ways; they kept themselves busy for hours just concentrating on their various problems. And this is exactly what they were doing on the morning of Agatha Bilke's arrival.

"Please welcome our newest addition to Ward Ten."

The staff nurse wheeled a mummy on a camp bed into the ward. The top half of the patient's body was now almost completely covered in bandages.

Agatha surveyed her new surroundings from under her mask. There was a small frieze of cartoon characters around the wall, a poster about trains and a photocopied sheet about health 'n' vegetables.

I won't be in here for long, she thought to herself. *I will leave before the authorities start asking questions, and then roam the countryside feasting off nuts and berries.* She was calmly noting the exit points when a ridiculous squawking ~~cockatiel cocktail~~ child walked up to her bed.

"Snooperb!"

What on earth was she talking about? Agatha could never have been described as "snooperb".

"Hello, I'm Cauliflower. Looks like you've been through the wars, eh? Electric shock, was it? Put your finger in the socket? Well, at least you're —" Cauliflower stopped and, like a very small eruption, but an eruption nonetheless, stuttered *"magnificent!"* very loudly. She ended with: "breathing!"

"Would you mind leaving me alone? I am trying to recuperate."

"Would you mind leaving me alone, please?" Agatha spat. "I am trying to recuperate."

Cauliflower looked intently at her splendid new friend.

"Let's help those in need, Agatha. I know the hospital inside out. You must come with me on my night-time rounds as I cheer up the frail and dying."

On hearing this, Agatha became interested (but only slightly). *She must know how to slip past matron.*

Normally, Agatha found it hard not to be malicious to other children, or adults, or officers of the law. It was in her nature to be rude and abrupt, but this time she knew she had to be clever. She couldn't risk making even one mistake. If she was found out she could end up in prison – which was unthinkable. To remain undetected, she would have to be nice to Cauliflower and anyone else she bumped into. Nice. Urgh. It made the hairs on the back of her neck stand up.

Agatha held out a bandaged hand. "Pleased to meet you."

Cauliflower pointed to the curtained-off area. "Holbeck Folbeck's in there. He's very rich, but he's – *choking!* – smoking, which is not very responsible."

At this moment the curtains parted, and revealed Master Holbeck, in his luxurious robe, puffing on a *Mitchum Lite*.

Agatha was entranced – she couldn't take her eyes off the boy. There was something absolutely magnetic about him. He looked so refined, so charming. Holbeck remained still, as placid as a lake – then, spotting Agatha, he gave her a wink. The smitten girl, wrapped up in a thousand bandages, tried to look mysterious and unattainable – here was someone she *did* want to get to know.

Matron Cakebread walked in. As the head of a busy children's ward she should have brought with her an air of both confidence and experience. Instead, she seemed somewhat confused.

5. PSYCHEDELIC CUPBOARD

"Good afternoon, er, children!"

It was as if Matron Cakebread didn't expect to see young people as she entered the ward. In her hands were what looked like a couple of old shirts and a packet of detergent. Matron composed herself after a moment and put her things on a convenient surface. The surface was not so convenient if you were Lynda Peanuts.

Cakebread took a bite from a large Chelsea bun and put it in her pocket. The children watched it ooze into the fabric of her uniform, which was straining against her figure. Matron was stout, rotund and not a little tubby — that is to say Cakebread had obviously been enjoying both. Often.

"Mental fleas!" shouted Cauliflower from the corner.

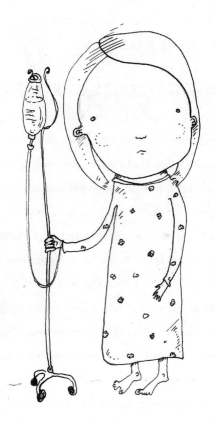

Lynda Peanuts was attached – literally and emotionally – to a drip

"As you are all aware," announced Matron, plumply. "The ward is full. Dennis Guffe – you were admitted 14 months ago. Holbeck Folbeck – it's been… too long."

The children looked at each other sheepishly. Even sheep would have been a bit surprised at how sheepy they all were. Even a chunky sweater would have been a bit taken aback, and that's saying something.

Matron Cakebread had been told in no uncertain terms by the Health Trust governors that if the children weren't getting any better she would have to do something about it. This was a hospital, you know, not a youth club.

"We are going to conduct thorough tests on all of you. Individually. We've got to find out what's going on. If you're not ill, you're out."

The children suddenly paid attention. Tests. Real, medical tests. Oh no. Each patient was going to be given various X-rays and specific examinations according to their specific complaints. There would be a short interview with the consultant and then ~~a great confrontation and loads of arguments and perhaps someone would get hurt~~ discussions would take place.

Cakebread was a woman whose twin passions – desserts and washing – had tended to hijack her thoughts when she should have been thinking about running her department.

She had been in the job for years and she was not as focussed as she used to be. Now, here was her chance to pick up the reins of this galloping horse of a ward and lead it into the 21st century! *Perhaps she would get a bonus and she could buy a new washing machine with a combined tumble dryer.*

"Come along, Dennis, you're first. Follow me to the X-ray room."

The patient slowly got up and put his slippers on, which looked like big fluffy claws. He was nervous. Was he going to be rumbled?

Matron smiled at him and they both walked out of the ward. Her anti-bacterial squirter hit the side of her hip as she did so, sending out small, hygienic sprays into the air.

"Pssst!" Someone was trying to attract Agatha's attention. "Pssssssst!"

It was Cauliflower, no doubt, so Agatha ignored it.

A finger poked her on the shoulder.

"Ow!" She turned around, incensed. "You do know I'm suffering third-degree burns-"

But the pest wasn't Trinkle at all – it was Holbeck. Agatha quickly smiled. Her knees fluttered, like moths who have seen a particularly handsome flame.

"Do you want to come and look at the psychedelic cupboard?" he whispered.

Agatha had never heard of such a thing – especially not in a hospital. She tiptoed after the well-to-do patient who was heading towards a nearby storage room.

Holbeck opened the door. Inside were boxes and boxes of medication. This room should definitely have been kept locked, thought Agatha, in a hitherto rare moment of maturity.

"Just imagine!" said Holbeck, pointing to the range of drugs on offer. "This one makes you happy, this makes you calm. This is excellent for quietening the voices in your head – and if you take this particular pill it *adds* voices."

Holbeck tapped a box full of tablets and smiled. Holbeck was as bad as she was. He was teasing her –

testing her mettle. She shrugged.

"And this last one," he lowered his voice. "Is good for the... *circulation*."

This time Agatha blushed. He grabbed another packet and threw it to her.

"Keep these," he said. "Might come in handy later on... sedatives – heh!"

The girl admired Holbeck but at the same time was a little scared by him. This was a notch up from her level. This was *really* bad behaviour.

"How do you know about all this stuff?"

"Agatha Bilke, isn't it? Mind if I call you Bilky?" Holbeck leaned against the shelves. "My mother has lots of pills and potions. Buys them from the Internet, none of it on prescription. Very tedious, really."

He coughed a bit and she listened.

"See, Bilky, no one has any *fun* around here. They're all too busy dossing around and pretending to feel ill. I can see that you're someone who really relishes excitement. Eh? Tell me I'm right?"

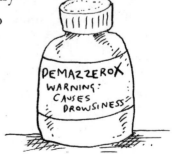

"Yeah, s'pose so."

Agatha was inwardly delighted. Holbeck was a wonderful boy. A triumph of anarchy. A marvel, a kindred spirit. And someone who was stinking rich! Hospital was not going to be boring after all. She felt he could sense the type of ~~barnacle~~ person she was immediately.

"How *did* you get those terrible burns, Bilky? Caught *playing with matches*, eh?"

Gulp.

The suggestion was that she was an arsonist, most definitely. But this was said without horror or distaste. Holbeck had guessed her past – and he seemed to find it thrilling. Agatha, now so comfortable in his company, was just about to tell him this and perhaps mention some details about her hatred of humankind (which she had swiftly assumed was just like his), when the door opened and a nurse burst in.

"Holbeck! And the new girl! Come out of there at once. What are you doing? You know this is beyond bounds."

"I'm so sorry," simpered Holbeck. "It's not Bilky's fault. Blame me; I'm the one who dragged her in here. I was just looking for something to – *aheuurgh!* – quell the pain a little."

"I'll have to have a word with matron, Holbeck. You can't self-medicate here."

The children returned to the ward, heads bowed. Agatha gave Holbeck a big grin. He grinned back and his teeth were white and even, like a film star's. She sighed and wished she'd known him forever.

6. A RETHINK...

It was the week before a particularly tricky exam when Holbeck Folbeck had suddenly stopped walking. He'd had to be wheeled around on a trolley that his nanny had made from a converted skateboard and an empty Nortnum's hamper left over from Christmas. The hospital couldn't work out what the problem was. Holbeck had no swelling, he was not allergic to anything nor did he have deep vein thrombosis. When he wasn't causing mischief, he sat in his hospital bed watching films that hadn't even been released in this country yet, deciding what sort of sushi to have for lunch.

The other children were similarly laid-back. In her diary, Lynda Peanut's typical day read as follows:

"*8.30am Breakfast. 9am Lounged around for a bit. 12.30pm*

Lunch. 1pm Borrowed Holbeck's PlayNation X-Boxxy 2000. 3pm Cakes (lots of them!). 5.30pm Dinner. 6pm Telly. 8.30pm Lights out."

Agatha was starting to like it here.

She had initially wanted to escape as soon as possible, but as she sat with her new friends she wondered why she would want to leave. She was hidden under her bandages – if any of the so-called authorities were to search the place for an errant child who had (accidentally) caused a helicopter crash they would not recognise Agatha from her police mug shot. They would think she was miles away, in a commune in the south of France, eating olives and sending blackmail letters to local businessmen. *Ooh, a commune. Mmm, olives...*

Agatha gazed at Holbeck's corner as he took another *Mitchum Lite* from the packet. The flowers were so very fresh, the goblets for his Wybeena so very polished. He even had a portrait of his mother, painted in oils, hanging behind him. She was standing in some stately drawing room, dressed in ruffles and bows. *She looks like the queen,* thought Bilke. *So sophisticated.* Holbeck glanced up.

"Fancy a puff, Bilky?"

Agatha had never been the one who needed teaching before. She had, up to now, written the rulebook. There

Dennis Guffe claimed to have dreadful
stomach pains, but no doctor had ever found the cause

wasn't anything she didn't know about being streetwise – flouting authority and all that. But now, as she had been in the psychedelic cupboard, she was wide-eyed. She felt like the country mouse who goes to see its hard-rockin' town cousin. In her own environment, yes, she did know a thing or two – but she was woefully out of touch with what was really going on. Starting fires was nothing when you could light a cigarette instead. She wondered, dreamily, whether Holbeck had any ASBOs.

Agatha took a careful drag.

It was like sucking burnt toads through a straw that was clogged-up with gravel, 'flu and nits. It was disgusting. Agatha bit into the tip so the smoke didn't get into her mouth and blew out whatever there was as quickly as possible. She didn't cough, but she didn't exactly look cool either.

"Mm, lovely."

Holbeck could see that she was a novice but he didn't say anything, his manners were impeccable. He smiled and looked at her for a long moment.

"You haven't got a friend in the world and you come from a deprived family."

Agatha was surprised – how well he understood her.

"Want to see something funny?"

It was as if there was no one else in the room but Agatha. Holbeck was really turning on the charm – a rebellious, naughty sort of charm. Cauliflower looked on, jealously.

Holbeck brought out a battered-looking leather wallet from his dressing gown pocket and took out a fifty-pound note. It was clear that he wanted to impress.

"I'm rich, Bilky, but don't let that put you off. I don't care about wealth, I don't care about position."

He struck a match and lit the note. Agatha could not believe it. She was enthralled by this charismatic heir.

The nurse charged in. "Holbeck! Stop that smoking at once!"

She gazed at the charred note in his hand.

"Badly-behaved!" shouted Trinkle.

"Whatever you're doing, enough! It's your assessment in five minutes so hand me those matches."

"There's internet access in the library," whispered Holbeck to Agatha as the nurse left. "Fancy a bit of web-surfing later on?"

"Maybe." Agatha wanted to keep an air of mystery about her.

"Let's hook up after dinner."

"Double bookings! Isn't that when you're having your tests, Agatha?" Cauliflower didn't want the girl to make any

more new friends. She elbowed Bilke in the ribs.

"I think you should stick with me," she whispered. "You don't want to get in with the wrong crowd. This boy is dangerous."

"I'm *happy* with the wrong crowd."

Cauliflower frowned. She was not going to lose her new playmate.

"Agatha is *my* friend. *Mine,* Holbeck. We want to cheer people up, to sing songs. We're going to help – *loveberts!* – humanity! After me, Agatha: *Help the sick and help the poorly / If you don't they'll die for surely*".

Agatha groaned. This was not making her look good. She had never had two people want to be her friend before. She'd only had *no* people wanting to be her friend, which was not the same. And anyway, she didn't need Cauliflower now. She didn't want to see the routes of the hospital because she didn't have to escape for the moment; she was quite at home where she was.

7. *KOWSHKERPING!*

Home – where you can't always put your feet up.
Home – where you can never watch what you like on
the telly.

And there's washing up to do, and cleaning.

The Rottington was better than Agatha's *real* home,
much better than *anyone's* home. Oh, how she wanted to be
in bandages forever! She might look a bit strange but she
didn't care.

Even her assessment was going smoothly. The burns
were very real and the consultant Mr Bymbi could see that
she had been badly affected by the accident.

"But at least you're on the mend!" he snorted, eyes like
ping pong balls in the middle of an international tourna-
ment. "Now, just a routine X-ray to check you're all right

on the inside and the job's a good 'un."

The patient stood in front of a large metal frame, as big as a lion but not as furry.

Kowshkerping!

The X-ray was taken.

"Kowshkerping!"

Agatha looked round. This time it wasn't the machine – it was someone mimicking the sound. She tried to see if Mr Bymbi was doing it but there was no one else in the room.

"Kowshkerping!"

That noise again. The door opened and there was Cauliflower, giggling.

"Kowshkerping it goes! *Kowshkerping!* It makes me laugh and laugh! My turn, Agatha Bilky-boo! Best Friends!"

The consultant rushed forward: "These tests are highly confidential, young lady, please wait until we call you in."

"But I just wanted to –"

"No no! Leave the room NOW!"

Bymbi was looking extremely concerned.

A nurse pinned the X-rays up on the light box and she looked worried too. As the consultant tried to squeeze Cauliflower out of the door, the loud-mouth noticed the problem straight away.

"Eeeeiiii! You don't have a heart!"

No heart? Agatha peered at the photo. She knew she wasn't always the best-behaved child but she had not thought that there could be anything physically wrong with her – even less that something inside her was actually missing. But the evidence was plain to see: she was heart-less. The X-ray clearly showed a pair of lungs, a big liver, a stomach and a couple of kidneys – but there were no other organs on display.

"You don't have a *hea-rt!*" sang Cauliflower. "You don't have a *hea-rt!*"

The atmosphere soured as quickly as it would in a hot

Kowshkerping!

yoghurt shop – although the adults tried to appear relaxed and casual.

"Hey! Nothing to worry about, Agatha! Some glitch, I'm sure." The consultant removed a small potato crisp from his ear and ate it. "You'll just have to wait for our health dossier. No probs. Hoo! Come on girls, it's been a long day."

He motioned them into the corridor.

"But what about *my* health review?" yelled Cauliflower. "I'm ready!"

"We've, um, run out of time now," he said. "Tomorrow morning, bright and early – see you then!"

He hiccuped in a way that made it clear that he didn't have the hiccups – that he was trying to lighten the mood. A mood that might be extremely solemn if they all sat down and thought about it properly. For the hospital to have a patient with no heart was a Serious Matter. What could humanity do with someone with such an enormous flaw – other than lock her up for infinity in Hopelessnessness Prison?

Bymbi had to think fast. Bilke would need constant supervision and she must be guarded at all times – surely she would wreak disaster wherever she went. Plagues of frogs, locusts and perhaps stick insects would descend on

49

them all if she was not monitored night and day. Having no brain is not a problem — there are lots of stupid people who are very happy and contribute to society in a very positive way. To have barely a soul is fine, if you want to go into advertising, but to have no heart — that was unthinkable. Agatha Bilke's life would never be the same again. The Rottington, too, would never quite recover.

But, for Agatha, the worse thing was that Cauliflower knew. What if she were to tell someone? Like Holbeck, for example. What would happen if he discovered the ghastly truth? She would just have to keep Cauliflower's mouth shut.

8. CODDLES' MIND

The next morning, Coddles was in his office at police HQ, sitting at his desk, which overlooked Rottington Manor tube station.

Coddles was sure he had heard stifled laughter from the crowd at the *Police Matters* ceremony. But he didn't want to dwell. There was a large piece of paper in front of him. On it was written "Helicopter Smash Up – My Ruined Entrance" and it included a list of suspects:

The man from the ice cream van.

Albert "I'm Mad" Fiddlesticks.

The park attendant who is a bit of a loner.

The woman who has all those cats down the road.

Me...

He had to pin the crime on someone, *correctly*, but he

was having trouble with this one. He had only added the last two names to make the list look longer. He scratched his nose.

"Cup of tea, Chief Inspector?"

Brian Peas, his new assistant, was standing in the doorway. He was short, a little flushed and had spiky gelled hair that gave the impression that his head had been freshly plucked from the Great Barrier Reef.

"You know they've solved the Funnel Road murders?"

"Really?" Coddles was taken aback. This case had been one of the trickiest Rottington had ever had. The leads all lead to... nowhere. What they needed to do was to join the dots – Leads United.

"Yeah, turns out this copper did it. Hat, narrowing eyes, big plaster on his conk. Inspector Coddles his name is, *hahahahahaaaaaaaaaaaaaahhhaaa!*"

PC Peas had a sense of humour that Coddles was finding increasingly irritating. He kept making jokes about important police affairs – and these jokes were not especially funny. The detective inspector sighed.

"Tea, Peas. White, one sugar."

"No, say it properly. Tea, please."

"I simply meant 'Tea, Peas'. It's your name."

"Tea, please."

"Oh have it your own way. *PLEASE.* Just put the frizzing kettle on."

Peas left. Back to the list. If only he could put the constable's name on it.

The senior policeman glanced out of the window again, only to see the figure of Margaret Bilke walk out of the tube. He recognised Agatha's older sister straight away. Who could forget such a sturdy girl? He wondered if she was still into robotics and pickled onion sandwiches. It was a long time since the two had first met – after Agatha had set her sister's dress on fire, if he remembered correctly.

Agatha Bilke.

Something must be very wrong, very wrong indeed, for Agatha's sister to be seen nearby. This was a bad omen. Coddles shivered like a lemon watching a very scary TV programme.

He noted all the recent crimes in the area: theft of a terrapin – no. Man found laughing near a lamppost... messy kerfuffle at the local comprehensive....

But of course!

He looked at the piece of paper in front of him. The helicopter crash. Ah.

Coddles grabbed his trench coat and ran downstairs. He had an inkling (and all good Chief Inspectors work on inklings) that if he followed Margaret, she would lead him to the culprit.

Coddles narrowed his eyes.

I must stop doing that, he thought.

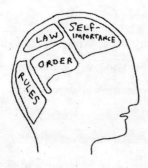

Coddles' Mind

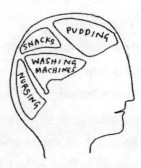

Cakebread's Mind

9. RICH PEOPLE

"We want answers, matron. And we're going to get them."

Cakebread had a lot on her (already rather large) plate. There were rumours that one of the young patients was wandering around at night, bothering everyone. Then there were the hospital governors sniffing around. And now it was only half past nine and Mr and Mrs Folbeck were already on her case.

"When are you going to cure my son?" Mr Folbeck was direct. "It's been a good many months now, Cakebread. Surely there's something you can do. He can't walk without a stick, for goodness sake."

Matron was shaky. The extra-double-chocolate woffuccino she'd had with breakfast wasn't helping. "We are awaiting the next set of results, then we shall ascertain exactly what is wrong with him."

She thought a word like "ascertain" would impress them, when a simple "find out" would do.

"He's had tests before, hasn't he?" Mr Folbeck, chewing a mint.

"Yes, but these ones are much more detailed."

"In what way, Mrs Cakebread? *In what way?* Tests are tests are tests are tests. He's had his knees examined, his ankles inspected, his feet analysed and his toes tweaked. He has had his ears syringed, his nostrils excavated and his arms have been given special Ayervedic cereal wraps. We have spent hundreds on his treatment, thousands even. And we just get more tests!"

Mrs Folbeck, who had been silent up till now, got up close to Cakebread. Her pink nose almost touched matron's sticky one.

"We may be rich but we're not thick," she sneered. "Get your consultant in here quick if you don't want to lose your most prestigious patient. My darling boy! Ruined by the quacks in this place!"

"It's a joke!"

"A shambles!"

"I will write to the head of the Reuters news agency!"

"And perhaps Kofi Annan, from the UN!!"

Cakebread was unnerved. Of course, whether a child was posh or not was irrelevant to her – she was here to help all kiddies, whatever their background. But she did not like falling out with the parents. She picked up the phone and dialled the consultant. Mr Bymbi arrived quickly. On rollerblades.

"Hello! Mr and Mrs Bilke. I am so terribly sorry." He clasped Mrs Folbeck's hands as if she was the last raspberry on earth and he was a small but hungry marmoset.

"I know this must be dreadful news and I'm sure Mrs Cakebread has tried to break it to you slowly... but we can't help the fact that Agatha has no heart. Please don't blame yourselves."

He took a long, deep breath.

"We're just going to have to protect society from her and keep her locked up at all times. All right? Good. Must dash."

"Who is this Agatha girl?" Mr Folbeck was quite confused.

"I can understand that you might be in denial right now but here is a pamphlet, *How To Cope When Your Child Is Discovered As The World's Only Heartless Human Being* which you might like to have a look at."

"No no!" cried Cakebread. "What Mr Folbeck means is that he is Mr *FOLBECK!* His son is Holbeck! These are not the Bilkes!"

Bymbi looked aghast. Patient confidentiality is the medical establishment's golden rule. A doctor should never disclose anyone else's details. *Ever.* Especially if the person in question is a danger to humankind.

"Just kidding!" said Bymbi. "Yes, er, so... Holbeck. Fine chap, Holbeck. Two legs – nothing wrong with them. Says he can't walk – making it up perhaps?"

"What? You think our son has invented his condition?"

"Just a thought."

"This is outrageous!" Mrs Folbeck was not pleased. "First, you seem to imply that our son is cruel and callous..."

"I only said heartless...."

"Well it's near enough. Then you have the cheek to suggest that he is not ill at all! Come on, Clement! We will be marching up to the governor's office right now!"

"Lord and Lady Fol-" Cakebread was simpering.

"You can't stop us, matron. We will report you and your so-called consultant. If we are not sufficiently impressed, we'll take Holbeck out of the Rottington. He can be treated at home by the finest doctors in the country."

Bymbi looked pleased to see them go.

"I can't stand wealthy people," he said loudly, as they padded out of the office. "Frizzing arrogant frizzers."

"*Language,* Mr Bymbi." Cakebread sighed. "We're close to losing ourselves a bundle of money. Their cash was subsidising the other children's treatment too. Not that they knew it…."

"We'll get by," said Bymbi, absent-mindedly polishing a rollerblade with his sleeve.

"But we have Agatha Bilke! The planet's worst child!"

Cakebread was in a mess. The Rottington was in a mess. Bymbi tried to explain to Cakebread that all was not lost, that something could be done to save Agatha – one day. "It isn't the first time we've had someone without a heart at the hospital," he said, brightly. "And it worked out fine in the end."

At this, Cakebread was excited. So there was a light at the end of this very long tunnel – a tunnel that at the moment smelt of old beans and mouldy horses.

"Who was this patient pray tell, Mr Bymbi?"

"Oh, I just invented that to make you feel better," said the consultant, strapping on some kneepads and rolling to the door. "Don't worry, matron, if the situation doesn't improve then we can always resign."

Bymbi tried to explain to Cakebread that all was not lost

Strangely, this was of no comfort to Cakebread. She was running out of hope. How had they arrived at this sorry circumstance? With Holbeck gone and this girl to contend with, she didn't feel she could manage. Pressure, that was it. Pressure on her temples, pressure on her ankles. Pressure in the centre of her back – shooting pains, difficulty breathing, tightness in the chest, stomach contracting, intense nausea – *the gnawing smell of woffuccino!* – back stooped – vomit – the shakes – collapse.

Matron had gallstones, although she did not know it, and she was having an attack. Eating too many rich foods and not taking enough exercise had been her undoing. As she fell to the floor Bymbi called for a stretcher.

10. HYPOCHONDRIA

Matron was wheeled quickly out of her office, gasping loudly and clutching her stomach. The patients barely noticed the drama as they discussed the increasing number of physical problems they were facing themselves. There is a word for this sort of behaviour, hypochondria – when someone believes they are gravely ill even though they just have a sniffle or a broken nail. The patients in Ward Ten were not aware that this condition had a name.

"Not only is my foot bad – I can't see a bean."

Holbeck was relating a tale about his weakening sight, not about his blindness to lentils. He waved his hand around dramatically. Agatha could see that he had a tattoo on his wrist, depicting an overweight eagle.

"I insisted that Mummy take me for an eye examination,"

continued the posh boy, unaware that his parents were in the building, kicking up a stink. "But *Rothmere-Goldsmith and Oxbridge* opticians – and they are the best in the country – informed me that I had perfect 20/20 vision. Unbelievable."

The children all thought they had good reason to stay at the Rottington. They hoped these tests they were having would prove this to be the case. Certainly, Dennis thought that if he just talked loudly enough he would be overheard and his residence at the hospital would be assured.

"I'm sure I'm autistic," he explained. "I saw a documentary about it. I can't relate to people but I can draw flies really well. All the bits in their eyes and everything."

"I'm dyslexic and hypoglycaemic," said Lynda. She turned to the arsonist. "And what about you? We can see that you've had a very bad accident, but perhaps you've got scurvy. People sailing the high seas used to get that, my dad said so. Just think, Agatha, you could be the first person in Britain to bring it back! Or perhaps it's gout."

Agatha was silent, but smiled wanly – as if the merest suggestion of illness weakened her immune system. Of course, she didn't want to mention the X-ray. No one must know about it. Cauliflower had already been warned and Agatha continued to stick a sharp pencil in her ribs to let her know that she was serious. She changed the subject.

"I would have thought you'd smoke a pipe, not *Mitchums*," Agatha said to Holbeck.

"Nah, it's cigarettes all the way with me, Bilky."

The children all cooed at Holbeck, because he was so worldly. All apart from Agatha, who just tried to look nonchalant. He winked at her again. Holbeck and Bilky were really getting on – like a house on fire, some would say. He had lent her his special propelling pencil, which told the time in Helsinki and which she was now using to threaten Trinkle.

Agatha had always suspected she wasn't quite right and up to now she had relished the fact: it had made her who she was. Her parents liked to argue and that was often her excuse for her irresponsible behaviour. But to have been labelled with a real, identifiable physical problem was dreadful, something she couldn't control. Soon she would be whisked off into some special unit and given more tests. Each part of her body would be documented in the tiniest detail and there would be lots of paperwork. Her parents would be told about the enormity of the situation and it would make them fight more. She'd have to sit in ~~wellies~~ the dark, probably, and eat health foods. Maybe the prime minister would turn up and lecture her about being a danger to society and tell her she would never return to normal life unless someone from the House of Lords got involved.

She would require salvation. They would make it a big moral case. She would have to undergo a lengthy operation to receive the heart of the Kindest Person In Britain – who would have died while saving a kitten from a bulldozer – and then the papers would get involved. Life would never be the same again. And all because of that X-ray! It all seemed so final. Would Holbeck disown her if – *when* – he found out about her condition?

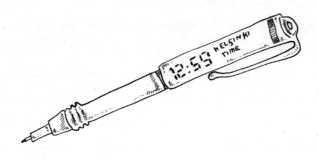

Holbeck had lent Agatha his special propelling pencil

"Holby, I'm thinking of getting a tattoo." She had to keep cheery. "What would you recommend?"

"Oh Bilky, you'd look great with an enormous skull and crossbones across your shoulder. And an axe near your lower spine. Perhaps a little machine gun on your ankle and a suckling pig on your forearm."

"Really?" Regarding body art, Holbeck seemed to know his onions.

"I know this excellent tattoo parlour. *Gainsbourgh, Constable and Whistler* do the most excellent work! They're in Jermyn Street. Near the Royal Academy. We'll go together next Tuesday – bunk off physio…"

The conversation was interrupted.

"Holbeck Picasso Byron Virginia Woolf Clement Folbeck III! You're leaving at once!"

Mr and Mrs Folbeck marched into the ward and started packing up their son's possessions. Agatha recognised his mother from the portrait, which must have been painted a while ago.

To Agatha's surprise, Holbeck did what he was told. She could not believe it. She thought that he would naturally disobey his parents, as he did the rules of the hospital. He glanced at Agatha and then turned away.

Perhaps Holbeck didn't know what to say because he

was going. But why should that make a difference? Bilke should confront him now – otherwise when would she see him again? Perhaps he would not be allowed to set foot in the Rottington ever again – and what about next Tuesday...?

Just as she started to approach him, a rough hand on her (fragile) arm pulled her back.

"A*aaa*gatha, what a state you're in!"

11. SQU*AAAA*SH

M argaret Bilke was surprised to see so many bandages on one head, let alone on two arms. She plonked her bag down on the bed and brought out a large yellow vegetable.

"I've brought you some squ*aaaa*sh."

This was not what other people meant by the word "squash" – that delicious fruity cordial you mix with water. This was a squash, a bit like a pumpkin. Not the same at all.

"My, they have b*aaaa*ndaged you up something proper," said Margaret. Again, she fished into her bag and took out a jar of pickled onions and a loaf of bread. She carefully placed the onions one by one onto a slice.

"So hungry! I was saying to mum…" Blobs of food plummeted out of Margaret's mouth like terrified mountaineers.

"…By the way she's not talking to Dad – but I said, 'I wonder if Agatha's been b*aaa*ndaged up good and proper?' Well there you go, you h*aaa*ve been. Pickled onion?"

Margaret had a habit of lengthening the "a"s of any given word so that it sounded ridiculous. Agatha watched as Holbeck collected the last of his belongings. She could do nothing to stop him leaving, it seemed. Her sister had barged in and ruined everything. For a second and last time, he had glanced up at her as he followed his horrible parents, clutching the oil painting in one hand and his mother's handbag in the other. Agatha tried to block out Margaret's dreary teeth and her monotone chatter. She was talking about her new samba classes.

"…It's so much better than robotics! My teacher says I could be the new Torvill and Dean. If I can find a Dean."

"They're ice skaters," said Agatha, sulkily. And then, suddenly: "Holbeck! Don't go!"

"Too late!" whispered a voice under the bed.

"A*aaaaa*gatha! Have you got mice?"

"*Quietkins!* I'm hiding!" murmured Cauliflower. She took a moment to realise that she had blown her cover and then crawled out from under the bed.

"Holbeck's seen the X-ray. He never wants to speak to you again."

"What?" Agatha turned white.

"Which X-ray is this?" asked Margaret, who was pleased to see that the voice came from a human, not a rodent.

"It's on his bed. I showed it to him just now. He was so ashamed that he once liked you."

Agatha's threats had obviously not had any effect on Cauliflower – or *enough* effect.

She ran towards Holbeck's bed and there was the X-ray, for all to see. Margaret ~~pretended to be a monkey~~ raised her eyebrows and continued to eat the sandwich, thinking this was just a childish spat between friends. No one had yet informed her about her sister's medical condition and she was more interested in onions.

And then – yes, *then* – Coddles appeared at the doorway, looking for answers.

12. ATTACK AND RETREAT

"Inspector Coddles!"

"Margaret Bilke!"

The policeman waved at Agatha's sister, gleefully, and then resumed his menacing glare.

"Agatha, I think we need to talk about the Helicopter Incident and the little fire at the park."

Margaret rushed up to him. "My sist*aaaa*h is above suspicion, Inspector. She doesn't do that sort of thing anymore, she told me that l*aaa*st week."

"That's as may be, but we still have to ask some very uncompromising questions. She looks guilty."

Before Coddles could start his inquisition, Cauliflower came hurtling along, fresh from her assessment. She spoke directly to the policemen.

"*Sheepy pie!* Thank goodness you're here. My name is Cauliflower Trinkle and I have a revelation about Agatha!"

Cauliflower's confidence was growing. She thought she was a law-abiding person, doing good.

"You see that girl has been led astray. She has no heart, unlike normal people, and thus is open to – *chorizo!* – influence."

Coddles did not even glance at Trinkle. He thought she was talking metaphorically, not literally. Of course Agatha was heartless – everyone knew that. But no one could be missing an actual heart, that wasn't physically possible.

"Yes, you're right," said Coddles. "She is horrid, manipulative, nasty. It's all written down in my notebook – but I have to ask Agatha about a significant crime, if you don't mind. Sit in your bed and look glum – that's what you patients do, isn't it?"

Mr Bymbi rolled into the fray and put a firm hand on Cauliflower's shoulder.

"I think you might be going a bit far there, Chief Inspector... You can't talk to the kiddies like that..." He spotted Agatha and put his other hand firmly on *her* shoulder.

"Aha! Our very own elephant man! We have a room we need to lock you in, er, a suite we'd like you to look at."

"I can talk how I frizzing well like!" frothed Coddles. "*I'm* boss. Now Agatha, you wretched puddle of pig-swill – I need to take you down to the station."

"I'm sorry," said Bymbi. "Agatha must stay here."

"No no, she has to come with me."

"No, under strict hospital rules – she *must* stay."

"I'm the police, we're more important."

"I'm a doctor, *we're* more important. Cakebread gave me strict instructions...."

"Dilemmas!" shouted Cauliflower.

She had hit the nail on the head. Who was the top dog? The law, saviour of the nation's morals and upholder of justice and peace, or the medical firmament? Which one could decide who was loony and who was most definitely not? Could one or both *really* save lives? Agatha might have been physically ill, or she might have been just bad. Perhaps no one would ever decide.

Agatha had to act immediately. She stuffed the X-ray down one of her slipper socks, grabbed Cauliflower by the collar and ran out of the door.

So Coddles wanted her banged up in prison and the hospital wanted to section her. She had to go to Holbeck and find out if he had seen the X-ray. The trouble was she had this unwilling accomplice with her. Then, at once, she remembered: Cauliflower knew the hospital inside out. Agatha stopped and gripped her ear.

"Get us out of this frizzing place!"

Cauliflower, who was genuinely scared, stuttered as she tried to remember the layout.

"But it's g- g- getting – *Pingu!* – dark!"

"It's *always* dark at night, that's when you said you traipsed around."

"Um, I only went to the OAP ward once and they're on the same floor as us."

"You gave me the impression you visited *everyone*."

"No, not really."

This was useless. They walked along the corridor until they saw light spilling underneath the door ahead.

"Goof! This is definitely the way out!" Cauliflower perked up.

They tiptoed up and tried to peer in. Then the door opened and they nearly fell forward. A booming voice greeted them.

"Doctor Corgi and Doctor Daschund! You've arrived! Good journey? Plane a bit late but never mind – golly, they said you were short but I didn't realise how short! And bandages! How novel. Tallinn is beautiful this time of year, is it not? Come, come – you must get your scrubs on and into theatre immediately. No time to lose! Our patient's gallbladder needs removing, *hahahahahah!*"

The girls were each handed a gown, hat and paper mask. Agatha could not believe it. She and Cauliflower were going to perform surgery – on a living (for the moment at least) human being! She wondered if they would have to fix an ankle, sew on a severed finger – or perhaps it was a boob job? Great. This was better than a box of matches any day. She looked at Cauliflower, who seemed a little nervous. They could find their way out afterwards.

"Mmm! Mm! Mmmmm!"

Trinkle was quivering and humming frantically to stop herself exclaiming.

The scrubs hid most of Agatha's bandages – it seemed they could both easily pass for a couple of the Eastern European doctors that the Rottington regularly brought over to perform routine operations because they were cheap. As the girls walked into the theatre Agatha tried to look authoritative; she was surprised at how bright it was. Someone switched the radio on and dance music blared out. The anaesthetists – one of whom was wearing day-glo jodhpurs and a smiley face t-shirt under his scrubs – were leaping about as they made sure the patient was "out like the proverbial".

"You've read the notes of course," continued the booming man. In the light he was obviously a very large bear dressed as a man. Or a man dressed as a bear. Or something between the ~~four~~ two.

"Simple laparoscopic cholecystectomy. Over in an hour or three. The patient is overweight, over-worked, under-paid and middle-aged. *Aren't we all!* Mrs E. Cakebread."

Agatha and Cauliflower looked at each other. They were going to operate on Matron!

The bad girl grinned behind her facemask. This was great. She couldn't wait to tell Holbeck. Before she took the scalpel to Cakebread's stomach, she said loudly:

"Doctor Corgi, could you stop that humming? I am trying to concentrate here."

"Frizz frizz frizz frizz frizz frizz frizz! Over-excitement! Nuts!"

"And please," said Agatha, as Holbeck's mechanical pencil toppled from its slot in her top pocket and accidentally fell into matron's pancreas, "no swearing in theatre, thank you."

The text on the bag reads:

SURGEONS
MEDICAL
SCRUBS

WOT YOU
WEAR FOR
OPERATIONS

He was obviously a very large bear dressed as a man.
Or a man dressed as a bear. Or something between the two

13. KIDNAP

It seemed that Agatha had successfully performed a routine gallbladder removal on Cakebread (if you can call dropping a writing instrument into the patient's belly "successful").

Indeed, "Dr Daschund" had been highly praised for such a quick operation – at twenty minutes it was surely a world record. "Dr Corgi" had not received such recognition, as he had had to leave theatre after two minutes on account of his uncontrollable, girlish swearing. After the event, Corgi and Daschund could be heard "having words" in the swab room.

Cauliflower wanted to go back to the ward, but Agatha told her she couldn't because she'd been kidnapped and that they were going to find Holbeck.

"So you *are* heartless!" shouted Cauliflower. "I don't

want to leave the Rottington. I like it here! *Chins.*"

"We're both going." Agatha had found a desire stronger than that which compelled her to light fires. She needed to be with Holby; this was a once-in-a-lifetime thing.

Cauliflower made for the door as Agatha scrambled after the girl and caught her legs just as she was reaching for the handle. Her knees were especially knobbly.

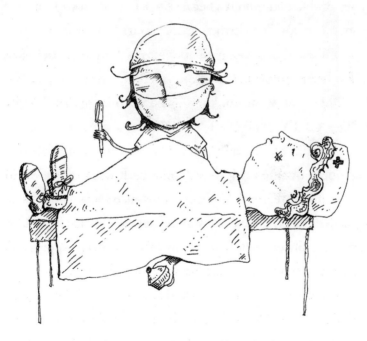

"Dr Daschund" was highly praised for such a quick
operation – at twenty minutes it was surely a world record

"Let me go!" screamed Trinkle. "I am not your hostage! You have just performed surgery on a fragile, old woman! You have hurt me a few times with a pencil! You have escaped from the police. I hate you! I can't believe we were friends in the first place."

"There was never a point where we were friends. You just have an over-active imagination."

"Holbeck ruined you! He gave you that cigarette! You are problematic and it's because of a boy!! And you, such an innocent young girl when you arrived… My friend! *Mine!*"

Bilke had had enough. This girl was completely deluded. She had to put her straight.

"Do you want to know who I am?" Agatha fumed. "DO YOU WANT TO KNOW? I am a fire starter, a bad person. I hate you and I hate everyone. If I *am* heartless… it doesn't matter as long as Holbeck likes me."

Cauliflower now looked calmly at Agatha. Her whole manner had changed; she was defiant. She wasn't scared, far from it. She snatched the X-ray from Agatha's slipper sock and brandished it.

"Holbeck wants nothing to do with you. He has seen the X-ray."

"You can't prove that. In fact I think you put it on his bed after he'd gone – just to scare me."

"I showed it to him, honest," said Trinkle. "I pointed at the big hole where your heart should be. It was the reason why he fled the Rottington so quickly. It's all over. I hope that you are sorry now, for all the pain you've caused me."

"You are a mean, stuttering, horrible girl. This isn't about *you* – this is none of your business!"

Agatha couldn't believe that this child, who seemed to be mildly eccentric on the surface, could be so selfish. She was simply jealous of Holbeck – and she would do anything to have her own way.

"I wish you'd get gangrene – over all of your body. And lumbago. And shingles and corns – *and* diarrhoea, mumps, leprosy! And *obesity*... *AND PILES*...

"If only you were *properly* ill," continued Agatha. "You should be made to suffer, like Holbeck has to – through no fault of his own. All that exclaiming and shouting is pathetic. You don't have a serious condition at all."

Cauliflower could hardly believe her ears. How *dare* she say that! She had not thought that Agatha was so rude, so disrespectful. For the second time, Trinkle started running for the door but Agatha now had her by the wrists.

There was only one thing for it. Agatha took the small bottle of pills that Holbeck had given her. *"Demazzerox – not to be taken unless under prescription. Causes drowsiness."*

She threw four tablets into Cauliflower's mouth and slammed her jaws shut.

"Swallow!" she jeered. "Swallow the tablets!"

Trinkle's eyes bulged a bit – but when Agatha prised her mouth open the tablets had gone. And it didn't take long before they started to work. After a bit of struggling the girl started to calm down. Soon she was asleep.

Agatha lifted Trinkle's clumsy body onto a handy stretcher on wheels. The one thing she couldn't do was get the sleeper's hand to let go of the X-ray, so Agatha covered her with a blanket. She would have to retrieve the evidence later.

Pushing the unconscious Cauliflower on the trolley ahead of her, Agatha set about finding her own way out. She'd keep Cauliflower hostage until she woke up, then stand her in front of Holbeck and force her to confess that she had doctored the X-ray to show it had no heart. The heir to the great mint fortune would realise that Agatha was not a freak and everything would be all right again.

14. FILING CABINETS

Bilke found the service lifts and went to the basement. There she waited in a corner with the trolley until she saw a porter pass. As he wheeled the bins outside, she followed him to the exit.

"Oi, you can't wheel a stiff out here, doc." He had a deep voice and very large nostrils. "You'll have to go to the mortuary."

"I'm zorry." Agatha tried her best Estonian accent. "I'm new here, couldt yout tell me vere that izt?" Perhaps from the mortuary she could find the exit. It was highly probable – no one would want to be in such a ~~vase~~ place for long.

The porter gave her directions and she was soon in a spacious, cool hall filled with what looked like large filing cabinets. But each drawer was not brimming with documents – this was where they kept the dead bodies. Agatha had seen it on television once – each corpse had a ticket attached to a toe. She wondered if she should take a look to see if it was true. She opened a cabinet. Carbon dioxide gas hit the back of her throat – it tasted like icing sugar but made her cough. There was a big, slightly flattened body in there – and a label which read "10894356". She shut the drawer and opened another right out. It was empty – at last, somewhere to put Cauliflower.

"I wouldn't do that if I was you." It was the porter again, who now seemed to have put a dinner jacket on over his uniform. "Mr Antipathy – pleased to meet you. This is reserved for a matron Cakebread, I believe."

What? Had the operation gone so wrong that Agatha had killed matron? Even Agatha – in her second case of thoughtfulness – now became concerned that she was taking things too far.

"Here. Pop 'em in." Antipathy showed her another empty compartment. On second thoughts, she couldn't really leave Cauliflower in the drawer...

"No, I zink I've changet my mind. Zank you, anywayt."

"What are you saying?"

"Er, I amz Eztonian?"

"No, not the accent. I don't know how they do things

where you come from, but we have to refrigerate the bodies. You *must* use the drawer. It will putrefy otherwise."

Mr Antipathy yanked the stretcher from the surgeon.

Agatha yanked it back.

The porter pulled even harder but she gripped it firmly. Under the blanket, Cauliflower's head wobbled but she remained asleep. With one last wrestle the porter got the stretcher. He lifted Cauliflower – still clutching Agatha's X-ray – and slid her into the great filing cabinet of the departed. The man turned round to smile and revealed a wooden tooth and a few loose screws. He locked the cabinet using a large set of keys that hung from his belt.

"See? No problem doc. Better scoot, eh? I'm sure you've got a truckload of surgery to be getting on with."

Agatha had no choice but to leave, and within seconds she was outside the Rottington, where she had wanted to be for so long. She had to go to Holbeck and tell him that, even though she didn't have a heart, she was still worth the effort. Perhaps his one heart would be enough for both of them. They would share it and be happy.

The night greeted Agatha like a brick hitting a light bulb. It was cold, brutal and grim. It was all very well saying she must get to Holbeck's, but she couldn't hitch a lift – what surgeon would do that? She couldn't walk, it was too cold, and she had no money for a taxi. The only vehicles around were ambulances...

Brilliant. Ambulances were spacious *and* she would be able to drive as fast as she wanted with the siren on. Agatha knew about cars, having driven last summer, twice, around a cul-de-sac. She found an ambulance with the keys still in the ignition. At no point did anyone ask what she was doing, they all assumed it was hospital business. There was one problem: the driver was asleep by the steering wheel.

"Mek way! Mek way! Urgent blood tranzfuzshun!" Shouted Agatha, yanking the man's sleeve and pulled him to the ground, where he flopped down happily, deep in his snooze.

Agatha climbed in, an odd sight in her bloody scrubs and bandages. She slammed the door shut and flicked through the street atlas, which had been lying on top of the glove compartment, until she found Peerage Avenue, the poshest street in the neighbourhood. If the Folbeck Mansion was not here, it wasn't anywhere. Agatha got into first gear and released the handbrake.

15. FAITH

Cakebread was alive — her drawer in the basement had been reserved for a worst-case scenario — but she did not like being in a hospital bed. Once a dedicated medical pro, she was now a patient. What a show she had made of herself — and all because of a few pastries. She really must pull herself together and get some sleep. But she couldn't, she was too anxious. And this was not aiding her recovery one bit. No no no. She wished she could dream about freshly-laundered petticoats and fabric conditioner but her mind was on Important Stuff.

Matron wanted to see her young patients, to take them through the assessments. How could she do that from her bed? She also had to see how the Dorey Wing was being transformed into the Dorey Secure Unit. Now that

Holbeck was gone it was to be converted so that it could house "the heartless one". No one else could provide help and support like matron, but for the moment she was powerless.

Poor, poor Agatha: a victim of her own biology! Cakebread was very enlightened when it came to judging the youth of today. She did not blame Agatha – or her parents or the schools or TV. Life was about chance – you didn't ask to be born and then you got what you were given. Agatha had drawn the short straw, so to speak. She had inherited her character; she had not chosen it. But children *could* be fixed, not exactly like water pipes or cars, but they could be rehabilitated. Through love. Lots and lots of love. Cakebread and her team had to be there for Agatha – hugging her, holding her and smiling at her early in the morning. They must tell her nice things about her handwriting or her dress sense to make her feel better.

Matron took to imagining ways to cure the girl; methods to get her back on the straight and narrow. She thought that Bilke might like to go to a washing machine seminar or maybe work with orphans in Africa. She might even be good at giving Ward Ten a new lick of paint. Something would work. Little did Cakebread know that Agatha had already received the best therapy in the country, at the TreadQuietly Clinic for Interesting Children – and that it hadn't had much effect at all. The senior nurse fantasised that one day she would open a commemorative fountain in the Rottington reception area, which would dribble Scotchland Spring water to the sick and needy. Agatha would be helping her. There would be an inscription behind them on a shiny plaque: "To matron Cakebread and St Agatha!" Or perhaps it should be: "To matron Agatha and St Cakebread!" Oh, to have a patient grow up and want to become a matron too! Cakebread smiled so broadly it hurt her stomach.

But what of the other children and their assessments? She wanted to break the news in person. According to Mr Bymbi there was absolutely nothing wrong with any of them, they were all perfectly healthy. Now she had to convince the parents that everyone was cured and their kids must go home.

A nurse came to check her blood pressure and refill the drip. She shoved a couple of tablets under matron's nose.

Ah, what a lovely drip. So secure.

Love. Love. It was all about love.

Lovely Rottington, Rottington Rottington.

"St Cakebread memorial"

*Matron would open a commemorative fountain in
the Rottington reception area, which would dribble Scotchland
Spring water to the sick and needy*

16. NICE

Agatha careered across the streets, accelerating very fast and then suddenly slowing down. This was not intentional, it was just because she didn't know how to drive very well. Fortunately, it was the middle of the night, so there was not a lot of traffic and she was less likely to crash into something. Furthermore, because people expect ambulances to drive erratically, as they're supposed to be getting somewhere quick, it was the perfect cover. The modern world. So fallible.

Agatha needed to plan what she would say to Holbeck. She had to prove that she could be nice. She would have to be nice with her elbows and her kidneys and her feet. She would be smart and funny, perceptive and open. She would also have to convince Holbeck that under the bandages –

and the surgeon's outfit covered with bits of old blood – she was ok-looking. She sighed. This was going to be quite difficult.

She would have to ask Holbeck directly whether he had seen the X-ray. But this wasn't very romantic and her current look did not exactly lend itself to candlelit suppers and sweet-nothings. Perhaps she needed to get on his good side – bring a gift.

What could she give the boy who had everything? She had some plasters in the back and an oxygen tube but she didn't think he'd want that. At the Rottington he'd needed a friend, someone to make trouble with. Had Agatha been born with a heart, it would have sank. Maybe he had only required a buddy, nothing more – yet Agatha had to admit that now *she* wanted more.

With Cauliflower left in the mortuary, Holbeck would just have to believe Agatha when she said that it was Trinkle who had meddled with the X-ray.

The irony was that Agatha wanted to tell Holbeck that she was normal – not a weirdo – but she knew that he liked her *because* she was different. Agatha was cheeky, nasty, rude, silly and fun. Being heartless – well, it added to the package. He might actually *like* the fact that she was not exactly ordinary.

Agatha was nothing if not extreme. Her crimes over the last few hours included threatening behaviour, evading the police, performing routine surgery without qualifications, kidnap, drugging a minor and leaving her for dead, stealing a vehicle, and even murder (hadn't she killed Cakebread?). Was this too much for Holbeck? Is that why he had fled – was he just *pretending* to be a bad boy?

The trouble was that if she decided to abandon her plan and go back to retrieve Cauliflower she would miss this opportunity to tell Holbeck that she deserved his love. However, if she wanted to show the boy how compassionate she had become she could hardly leave their fellow patient for dead or she would be a fake.

But Agatha was nobody's fool. She paused for a moment – a *white lie* wouldn't hurt anyone, would it? What if she were to ask Holbeck to help her save Cauliflower – who had *mistakenly* been trapped in the mortuary drawer? He would be none the wiser and she might even look heroic.

Rottington Rottington.
How many streets,
And birds that tweet,
Till I get to Holbeck
And tell him I'm not completely heartless and mean and vile?

Agatha needed some sleep. There were too many voices in her head.

"*Aaaaaaaaaaaaaargh! Heeeaaaalp!*"

Another one. Wouldn't it just go away?

Margaret Bilke, fresh from her samba class and feeling as light as a feather, was hopping across the road in order to get her bus. In the subsequent hit-and-run accident, her leg was run over by a wayward ambulance.

17. HUMBUG

Peerage Avenue was the most exclusive address in the neighbourhood. It was home to ministers, footballers and TV presenters. No house was worth under £10 million and all were conspicuously decorated to show the wealth of the occupants. Each residence looked as if it was a theme park in itself and at night the houses were lit up extravagantly. One was built Egyptian-style – a large statue of a Sphinx guarded the pyramid-shaped garage and there was gold brickwork everywhere. A few archaeologists milled around, sifting through rubble. Another house was covered in diamante and had luxury shops, a pizzeria, nail bar and a canal in the grounds. There were diamond watches in place of plants in the front garden. One mansion was based on a cruise ship, with portholes for windows and a funfair on the

Peerage Avenue

starboard side. A man was singing cocktail jazz badly from inside and someone else was shouting, "Shut up, Sir Froobisher!" quite loudly. The whole road was like Christmas. Lit up, full of treasures, happy times. ~~Disgusting show of riches, really.~~

The house opposite the cruise ship was painted a light green colour, and on either side of the large, wrought iron gate stood pillars topped with eagles. The front door was cream with a brown marbling effect like a humbug. This was the one, the Folbecks' Mansion.

Light was coming from an open attic window; everywhere else was dark. Agatha looked at the clock on the ambulance dashboard. It was half past midnight. She could only hope that the light was spilling out of Holbeck's room. Somehow, she had to get his attention without waking the whole house.

What she ought to do was creep, stealthily, into the garden and climb up a drainpipe. That's what they did in films but she didn't have much experience of this – the only drainpipes she had come across were usually in the process of melting under the hideous weight of many flames.

Agatha started walking up the drive, but this turned out to be carpeted with a thick gravel of mint imperials. The sweets crunched under her feet, giving off a strong smell.

Surely she would be drawing attention to herself by this alone – it was an effective substitute for CCTV. There was nothing for it but to slip under the hedge and go round the back. She could now add trespass to her list of crimes.

18. FLEAS

"I'll look into it. Of course, no problem."

Coddles slammed the phone down. It was the fifth call today. *Another* fire – this time in the south end of town. The policeman had been inundated with information since that Bilke girl had escaped. People were reporting catastrophic ~~blazers~~ blazes in Rottington left, right and centre. What was going on? Furthermore, the hospital had just admitted to him the results of Agatha's X-ray. *This is going to turn into a public relations nightmare when it gets out,* thought Coddles. How had he let her run away?

Rottington Rottington. What a hell of a place.

"Frizz!" he said out loud.

"More leads, boss." PC Brian Peas walked in with a stack of papers that made Coddles feel a bit sick. Why now, why here? Surely Agatha could not have done this much damage in a few hours. Or could she? Unless the whole nation was suddenly on fire, through some strange quirk of fate... It could happen. Hadn't everyone in Norwich had the same dream about an octopus on July 17th 2003? Or had he not remembered that correctly? ...He really should check his facts.

"Could you get me the newspaper archive from summer 2003, Peas?"

"Please."

"Peas."

"I said *please*..."

"PEAS."

"Plea-"

"JUST GET ME THE FRIZZING PAPERS, PEAS!"

Coddles needed a lie down but his stomach was rumbling. How would he find Agatha Bilke? He pondered this as he nipped out for a snack.

"Get matron Cakebread on the phone," he said to the man in the deli who had just made him a pickled onion sandwich .

Coddles needed to concentrate – he grabbed his meal and ran straight to the hospital. He mustn't let his mind play tricks on him.

He found Cakebread in a wheelchair, eating a box of *Folbecks' Deluxe Superbio* mints that Holbeck had left behind. She was parked next to Margaret Bilke who was in bed with her leg in plaster.

"Coddles!" Matron was furious. "Where is Agatha Bilke?"

"I'll be suing the Rottington!" exclaimed Margaret. "A*aaaa*nd the police!"

Coddles was not fazed by the ladies' protestations.

"The reason I am here is so I can find the exact where-abouts of Agatha Bilke. I shall be conducting a series of intervie-"

"And I haven't even *mentioned* Cauliflower Trinkle. Where is *she?*" Matron pointed her finger at the policeman. "This is a disgrace!"

"Both girls were in your care, matron, not mine." Coddles did something clicky with his teeth and thought how there should be more laws in this country to stop people being so irritating. "Patients are, officially, your responsibility. Still, this is a case for the big boys. Fires are springing up all over town and I, Coddles, will find Agatha and pin this all on her!"

"You don't h*aaaa*ve any evidence!"

Matron wheeled up to the Inspector.

"If you are going to be so heavy-handed we will do the detective work ourselves," hissed Cakebread as she rolled over Coddles' foot. "We *know* the girls and shall find them. You won't get any more information out of us!"

19. LIZARDY…

Holbeck's back garden was fit for a king. Or two kings, or even nine. There was a moat around the house, a maze, three tennis courts, a swimming pool, a drive-through burger bar and a special mint bed. A great many varieties grew there: peppermint, spearmint, watermint, orangemint, Japanese shoe-mint, chocolate doughnut-mint, dry skin-mint, mint-mint and mint-mint-mint. There was a large plant in the centre of the ground, marked *The Folbecks' Special*. It was leafier than the rest, and when Agatha came near it the smell was overpowering. It combined the leathery pong of a wallet with the sharp aroma of caviar and a subtle whiff of aftershave – all in a minty way.

She looked around for a shed filled with useful tools. The garden stretched way back, but there didn't appear to be

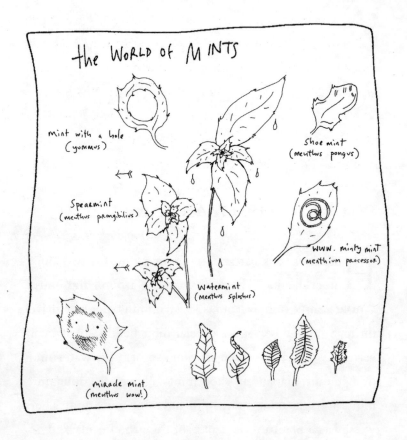

the WORLD of MINTS

mint with a hole
(yummus)

shoe mint
(menthus pongus)

Spearmint
(menthus prongibilius)

www. minty mint
(menthium processor)

Watermint
(menthus sploshus)

miracle mint
(menthus wow!)

one. So instead she picked up a mint and tried to throw it at the attic window. No luck. Too far up.

Maybe she should impersonate a howling cat to get attention.

Agatha glanced down and saw a load of butts on the floor – plus a lighter. Holbeck must have thrown them out of his room when he had finished with them. Many were only half-smoked. Maybe she could light a cigarette and waft the smell up towards his window. This was an inspired idea.

For only the second time in her life Agatha lit up a *Mitchum Lite*. It was repulsive. The toads were gone but the whole experience was a bit more lizardy, a touch manure-y. She started to splutter and cough.

"Achurrgggleurgh! Achurrgggleurghhhh!!"

At once, the drawbridge descended.

"Shhh, Bilky," said a voice from the darkness. "You'll wake the neighbours. Please do come in."

(A howling cat)

20. THE MANSION

All this time, Holbeck had been lurking in the back room, which was as big as a DIY superstore, watching Agatha explore the garden from the window. He hadn't been in the attic room at all.

The place was dark and in a mess. Holbeck himself was a state; his skin looked blue and his hands were shaking. He reclined on a chaise longue and closed his eyes.

Bilke hadn't quite expected this. He didn't look particularly pleased to greet her and it was only a few hours since they had last been with each other. Perhaps he *had* seen the X-ray and wanted nothing to do with her. Had Cauliflower had been telling the truth after all?

"Let's open a bottle of Vervois Boublé, eh?" But the boy said this blankly, as if he did not care one way or another.

Agatha looked around. The room must have been magnificent once – but now everything was covered in dust. Paint was chipping off the skirting boards and the furniture – which had obviously once been grand – looked old and musty. Holbeck appeared to be as tired as his surroundings. He rang a small bell and waited. Then waited some more.

"Seems like Vickers isn't bothering to take my call. No change there," said the boy. "He's probably sitting in the attic, reading his motoring magazines."

So that explained the light coming from the top room.

Holbeck seemed different – bitter, curled up at the edges. He clutched his stomach and gave an almighty yelp. The sound came from the centre of the earth – like a wolf that had been forced into very tight trousers.

"I'm not well. Not well at all."

Agatha had not spoken up till now. She never imagined that Holbeck would be like this. She thought he'd be tucked up in bed, being fed truffles by Vickers (if indeed Vickers was his servant), watching telly and having his toes massaged. Instead, he appeared to be living in a pit of his own making. And now she could see that unlike in the Rottington, where he had been in robust health, Holbeck did appear to be genuinely ill. Agatha didn't know quite where to start.

"So... how have you been?"

A flicker of pain crossed Holbeck's face.

"I think I've maxxed out all my mother's credit cards. One bottle of champers too many."

Holbeck's parents didn't seem to be around to witness their son's distress. Where were they? This chaos had to be caused by more than just ordering a few things on a store card. Perhaps the family was in big financial trouble. Perhaps the money had run out. Money has a habit of doing that, if you spend it on nice stuff ~~and enjoy yourself and forget about the bills by mistake but you didn't mean to really and you will pay the loans back, soon. Ish.~~

"Holby, are you all right?" Agatha was worried for the boy, but she was also concerned for her own feelings – Holbeck didn't seem to be interested in her. There was no spark there, nothing to indicate the close friendship they'd had at the hospital. She felt a small pang near her lungs – a yearning to reach out to Holbeck and comfort him. But only a bit, if he was going to behave.

"Say, what?" The boy tried to look lively, perhaps sensing Agatha's discomfort. "Do you want a tour of the old place?"

He grabbed his walking stick and hobbled over to the door. "Come with me."

Holbeck appeared to be as tired as his surroundings

She saw the Oriental ballroom; the Edwardian-style bedroom suites; the underground car park which doubled as an opera house; the thermo-water-power spa 'n' mini Icelandic geyser; a revolving restaurant and the home cinema room (complete with bored usherette who sat in the corner, chatting on her mobile). There was the mint-themed funfair – one ride involved being squirted by a giant tube of toothpaste while trying to wade through a river of teeth.

Lastly, they went to Holbeck's floor. Agatha had a box bedroom at home, which had a stack of her dad's unfinished Aerofixx kits blocking up part of the window. She had an old duvet cover with a ship on it and some fruit gums on the side table.

In Holbeck's suite there was a gold-framed picture of an aeroplane on the wall. "I'm getting my pilot's license next spring." His sheets were satin ("good for the hair, no static"); his curtains were made from the finest brocade with pictures of small emperors on them. Over the bed hung another painting of his mother, by Lesley Shins – the most famous modern artist working today. It didn't look like her at all.

"Worth around one mill," he said as he picked up a *Supermenthe Swirlwois* from a cut-glass bowl and popped it in his mouth.

Agatha had never seen luxury like it. Surely Holbeck was the richest child in the universe. And yet, as he showed her the wealth and finery in his home, he was not enthused. There was an underlying indifference to it all. What was wrong with him? How could she make things better? Should she coo at the hundreds of computer games he had? Or laugh at his jokes (if he decided to make any)? Perhaps not. Agatha, for all her faults, was not a sycophant, impressed by riches or status. She would have to be honest. If they were going to be friends – or perhaps *more* than friends – they would have to be straight with each other. She needed to discuss the X-ray. And then perhaps mention the fact that Cauliflower needed saving, and quick.

Holbeck coughed and wobbled a bit. Agatha remembered the Folbecks promising that he would receive treatment from the nation's greatest medics when he got home. Maybe they were stuck in traffic somewhere, arguing about kneecaps.

"Mint?" Holbeck offered Agatha the bowl and his manner suddenly changed.

"Do you like mints as much as they do in Chapel-On-Le-Frith? Or as much as Westward Ho!?" He threw the sweet in the air and caught it in his mouth. "Or is your intake as colossal as that of the small Scottish island of Eigg? I must repeat myself, do you *like* mints?"

Holbeck stressed the word "like" – he did not use the word "love". If he knew she had no heart he might be testing her. She might be able to like but never to love.

"I quite like them, yes." This wasn't a fun conversation; this wasn't about smoking or broadband access. She started to feel uneasy.

He whispered. "Shall I show you the secret room?"

Was this another trick? Coddles might be sitting in the corner, filling in forms that would see her locked away forever. Mr Bymbi might have the straitjacket ready. She would never see her parents again; she would never have a chance to live a full and free life. But it couldn't be a trick; Holbeck was not like that, was he? Unless he had been forced into it.

Agatha, a heartless mess of emotions, was changing. She wanted to be back with her friends in Ward Ten. She was sentimental, she was fond... all the things she had hated before. But this child and his money would not humiliate her, she resolved. If he didn't want her anymore she had no heart that could be broken.

As Holbeck pressed one of the sweets in the centre of the bowl, the gold-plated rococo bookcase slowly opened to reveal a vast room on the other side.

Still in her bandages, which were frayed and dirty, Agatha took a deep breath as Holbeck waved her through.

21. EMERGENCY

Life is random. Loads of things happen one day, then nothing the next. People you haven't seen in years all turn up outside the local grocers one week; then months later your pen stops working. All completely without rhyme or reason. But Cakebread had been enjoying more than her fair share of thrills recently. Yes she had been ill – gravely ill – but at least things were interesting. She smiled to herself as she wheeled out of the Rottington and into the community. She was a woman on a mission.

Matron had to find the two girls, whatever it took. These were trying times, she thought eagerly, as she rode over a bump on the pavement and nearly went headfirst into a recycling bin.

At first, it had been hard to know where to start, but

then Cakebread had decided to ring Cauliflower's parents and tell them she would be interviewing them pronto. At this point, she was not sure that the girls were mixed up in this fire business – as Margaret said, there was no evidence – but talking to the Trinkles seemed a good place to start.

Agatha's sister had also put matron straight on a few other matters. She had admitted that Bilke junior did have a history of starting fires, but "h*aaaa*dn't done it for yonks". She had told the head nurse where Agatha liked to go: the park, the boot shop, and the allotments... But Bilke Junior, they decided, could hardly have got very far with all those bandages wrapped round her.

"She is so very noticeable," said Matron, who had no idea that it was Agatha who had performed surgery on her.

"And th*aaaa*t shouty girl," said Margaret, who had no idea Agatha had run her over. "You can he*aaaa*r her a mile off."

Oh yes, that pair would stick out a mile off; this case would be solved in no time. Margaret offered Matron a courgette to take with her on her way to the Trinkles, in case she got hungry, but Cakebread declined. Her appetite was still small after the operation.

22. BLINKING

Agatha Bilke was not, as she had feared, confronted in the secret room by the police but by an enormous map of Britain on the wall, complete with flashing lights. It looked like it belonged to a Saturday night TV programme.

The map loomed over the two children as Kendall started blinking ferociously and Cardiff fizzled out altogether. The lights in Walsall were steady and strong, but there was nothing at all in Burnage, not a flicker. Holbeck pointed to the map with his walking stick.

"And this is the London Borough of Rottington! At least two happy customers!"

If she had been in any doubt as to what this meant, Holbeck soon made it clear.

"We can monitor every person in the country! Each

time they have a *Folbecks' Mint* we know, every time they share a packet with a friend we can spot it. Even if someone buys a gift tin in a service station in Cornwall and drives up to Inverness to give it to a favourite aunt or uncle – we have it logged."

This was the most animated Agatha had seen Holbeck all evening. He looked at his garnet-studded watch.

"It is 04.05 GMT and people are still enjoying *Folbecks'*. They will continue to do so tomorrow, and the day after that, and weeks and months after that. To think, I come from a family who have built up a reputation as the most popular mint-makers in the country! Aunt Clarissa – suffragette and originator of the *Extra Strong Folbeck!* Great Grandma Eugene – pioneering landscape gardener and creator of the *Chewy Folbeck!* Ah, it makes me feel proud. People will always want mints and they will always want the best: *Folbecks'!!*"

The child was fierce. His eyes burned with a passion that Agatha had not witnessed before. From a frail, abandoned little boy he had become a fuelled, patriotic standard-bearer for his parent's sweet company. She had previously thought that he didn't like his family – that he was a rebel – but here she had never seen loyalty like it. And his pride was making her feel small. *Her* family name had achieved

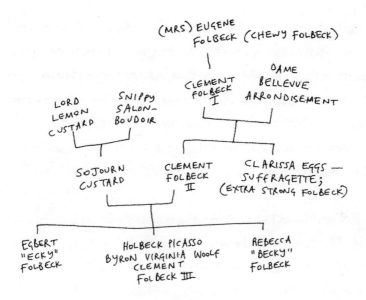

Holbeck's family tree

nothing. She had a grandad who had won some medals for having a shiny parakeet but no more than that. Her nearest and (not at all) dearest were always fighting amongst themselves, drinking too many ~~delicious ciders~~ energy drinks, not eating enough green leafy vegetables and hiding from the TV licensing van. Agatha, in the eyes of her parents (plus the law and society as a whole), was a failure. From the older generation she had inherited only big feet, a temper and now, it seemed, some sort of invisible/missing-organ syndrome. Her genes were far from noble.

Holbeck, she now realised, felt he was someone who mattered in life. He was not an unfortunate soul. He was heir to a vast fortune and, most probably, ~~a continent~~ contentment. But more importantly, he still had a sense of self that had not been damaged some way or another. He would grow out of this phase; go to public school, university... then into the family business. The scales removed from her eyes, Agatha confronted him.

"Have you seen the X-ray?"

Holbeck's attention was elsewhere. "Look! Someone's just eaten a humbug in Doncaster! You see every packet is fitted with a microchip. It's a bit illegal but very clever. No one will know and you won't tell, will you Bilky?"

"Holbeck, listen to me. *Have you seen the X-ray?*"

"Oh that old thing," said the boy, who was paying little attention to Agatha. "Aha! Another one in Scunthorpe! Hey, a couple have stopped chewing in Whitehaven – *frizz it.* Yeah, the X-ray – they said it showed no damage to my foot at all but it was definitely wrong. My toes are *very* painful."

"No, Holby. Did you see *my* X-ray?"

"Oh yeah, my parents told me about it. Mr Bymbi explained it to them by accident when they were in the Rottington."

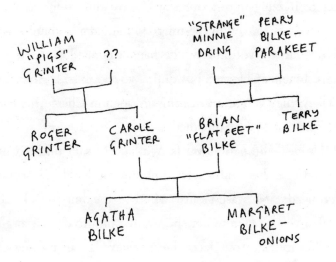

Agatha's family tree

"What?" Agatha froze. So he did know. It explained everything. Their friendship was worth nothing. She shouldn't have come here; she was foolish to think that she could rescue the situation. Holbeck was still wrapped up in himself.

"And so I told them, 'Mater and Pater, if the good doctors of the Rot. can miss out a whole organ on Bilky's X-ray, then they can miss out the problem with my foot. Simps. They believed me: case closed. The Health Service is full of frizzing idiots. But now I have this cough as well. When I last looked in the mirror I looked a bit blue – do I look blue to you, Bilky? Perhaps we need some liquid refreshment. Cheer us both up – you look so serious, Ag. Crikey, they've got a *Ceremony* tin open in Chesterfield! At this time of night! Splendid."

Holbeck limped towards Agatha. He said nothing but leaned over her and started untying the bandages around her head. She wasn't sure whether the burns had fully healed yet – and whether she wanted him to do this at all.

"Let me see your face," he whispered. "Let me see the real Agatha Bilke."

This was uncomfortable. Agatha had been cornered – but not by an irate Inspector or an overweight matron. As Holbeck unravelled the dressings, leaning ever closer, he puckered his lips. *He doesn't really care about me*, thought Agatha. *He doesn't want to get to know me. He is high on self-importance and his moronic mint empire.*

"Mummy says I need to find a good woman. Mummy knows it's important. But this girl's got to be right, got to be perfect for me. Would you like to meet my mother, Bilky?"

He slowly took the last bandage from her chin.

"You have very beautiful lips," he said.

"I'm not sure —"

"Shhh!" he put his finger to her mouth.

Agatha was petrified. Petrified that Holbeck might want to kiss her — she had not imagined that their first smooch would be like this. In fact, at this precise moment she wanted to run away.

"Stop it! Stop it! Cauliflower needs rescuing from the Rottington mortuary — she's been left in there for dead! I did it — I mean, um, I'm not an *awful* person. I shouldn't have left her in there, it just happened."

She'd blurted out the horrible truth. Would Holbeck like her now? He looked slightly baffled — his romancing had been interrupted.

"I should have never come here," Agatha could not stop blathering. "Join me if you want. There's an ambulance outside and I'm going now."

"Well that sounds like a jolly jape. Anyway, about this kiss…"

"Behave, posh boy." Agatha was resolute. "Either you come with me or you sit in this squalor until your parents come home."

Agatha ran out of the room and down the stairs, the posh boy limping after her.

23. AGATHA BILKE IS DEAD...

Mr and Mrs Trinkle opened the door like two accident-prone eggs which had just seen a drunk poodle driving a juggernaut. They invited matron into their small front room, where there was a tartan carpet and crystal figurines in a case.

Sitting on the sofa was Inspector Coddles. *Dammit*, thought Cakebread.

"Tea?" asked Mr Trinkle.

Mrs Trinkle glanced at her husband nervously as he went into the kitchen. She looked like she'd been crying for a while.

"Don't worry!" said the Inspector, trying to reassure her and assert his authority at the same time. "We're the police! We solve stuff all the time! Do you watch

Grime Crime Kiddie News?"

The worried mother nodded.

"Well it's not like that at all! Mostly babies stuck up trees. Um, I'm sure Cauliflower is alive and well."

"Aherm," said Cakebread. She did not like being ignored.

"I was here first," muttered Coddles.

The head nurse could not believe how rude he was. She wanted to thwack him across his nose but had to restrain herself.

"Could the girls, perhaps, be hiding here – in the house?" Coddles continued. "Happens all the time. That would be a turn up, eh?"

The policeman stomped upstairs to Cauliflower's room with his notebook. It was time for Cakebread to ask Mrs Trinkle sensitive, gentle questions. Just to gain a little understanding of their girl, and her friendship with Agatha. She would play the parents like a piano, she thought.

With tact, loveliness and diplomacy, Cakebread soon coaxed all sorts of details out of the Trinkle parents. She found out that Cauliflower liked going to netball practice – to cheer on the team – and that she collected sparkly pens. *How nice,* thought Cakebread. *But this doesn't quite help me with my enquiries.*

Mr and Mrs Trinkle

Coddles descended abruptly.

"Does your daughter like starting fires?" he asked.

"No! She's more interested in helping others – she's a selfless person, Mr Coddles. She might shout sometimes –"

"Well I'm sure she'll be back soon." Coddles did *not* seem sure. He was thinking how easy it must have been for

Agatha to have taken advantage of young Cauliflower. They were obviously roaming the country, setting everything alight. It was a mixed-up world gone loony.

Coddles' mobile phone started ringing and everyone jumped. He answered, hummed a bit, and then sighed.

"I have some important news," he announced, almost with some personal pride. "It could affect your daughter's situation…"

He sighed, paused for dramatic effect and made a noise with his throat much like the noise of a small dog eating meringues.

"Agatha Bilke is dead."

24. ...OR PERHAPS NOT

Agatha tried the ignition one more time but the ambulance wouldn't start in the cold morning air. Holbeck got out and tried to find the bonnet. There wasn't one – the engine was underneath the chassis.

"Bilky, I don't know if I can fix it." He continued to cough.

All around Peerage Avenue, curtains were twitching. Who were these strange medics? Was this private health care or that awful public-funded thingy? Illness in The Avenue would probably bring down house prices.

Holbeck wheezed a bit more and hit the side of the vehicle with his walking stick. He began to look a bit purple and suddenly fell over. He was out cold.

"Holby! Are you all right? Are you awake?" Agatha didn't

know what to do. He had fainted, or something worse – he might be in grave danger.

At this point a man in a smart suit walked briskly up to her.

"What's going on? Is everything all right?"

"Ve 'ave goit zings under ze control," said Agatha. "Ve are goingt ze hospital."

"Ooh, I'm due at the Rottington for a check-up, the car's in the garage and I can't be bothered to use public transport because it's full of ugly people," said the man excitedly. "Can I get a lift?"

"Ve can't ztart ze ambulanttze," said Bilke.

The man took one look under the chassis, removed a stethoscope, and fired up the engine. "I am the CEO of Platinum Motors," he explained. "I know all about cars." They strapped Holbeck into the back and the man then got into the passenger seat while the girl attempted to drive.

"Argh! Mind that cat!" said the terrified passenger, wishing he *had* caught the bus instead.

Holbeck needed medical attention, thought Agatha, that was for certain. Only now, as she was driving through red lights, did she have time to reflect. Holbeck may have overstepped the mark, leering over her like that, but he was in genuine trouble. He was not well and she had been too self-involved to notice that he needed help. And what had Cauliflower ever done to her? Nothing. She was kind and good and now she might be actually, properly dead because she was locked in a refrigerated drawer. Agatha was starting to feel ashamed of herself. Yes, Agatha was beginning to feel something.

She slammed on the brakes as they arrived at the hospital main gate and the ambulance lunged forward into a concrete pillar.

Mr Platinum Motors ran off to reception only stopping three times to wipe his brow with a handkerchief and once to vomit in the water fountain.

When Agatha opened the vehicle's back doors, Holbeck was still unconscious. She tried to get the oxygen unit to work but only succeeded in pulling it off the wall of the interior.

She had to get Holbeck into A&E, and then find Cauliflower and get her out of the mortuary. There was no way she would escape this time, she was resigned to it. She would become the medical improbability the Rottington had always been waiting for. Perhaps, she thought, she deserved all she got.

25. THE SEARCH IS ON

An ambulance was missing, so Cakebread had been told. It must have been Cauliflower's escape vehicle. They had found Agatha in the mortuary drawer, clutching her X-ray and, although they had not checked to see if she had stopped breathing, she had been pronounced dead. What no one could explain was these strange fires which had started in Rottington and were now countrywide – cropping up in places such as Leamington Spa, Cheadle Hulme and Yeovil. If Agatha hadn't been able to start them, had Cauliflower taken over as chief arsonist? Could she have got that far? Maybe Agatha had taught the girl all about fire-lighting and sent her on her way.

"But this doesn't tell me *how* she died!" sobbed Margaret as she was comforted by Cakebread in their ward. "I want *aaaa*nswers, Eleanor, and I'm not getting them! I'm going to sue the council! Or was I going to do that already?"

Matron was feeling the strain. The Trinkles kept ringing her, asking for news of their beloved daughter. Coddles was not helping either. He had forgotten about Cauliflower and kept banging on about Agatha's powers beyond the grave – believing that she was starting fires telepathically.

The lunch bell rang and Margaret looked up to see a large plate of minced lamb curry 'n' toast (one of the Rottington's specialities) heading her way.

"Oh! I c*aaaaa*n't eat!"

A louder bell sounded.

"All right, we heard you the first time," muttered Cakebread.

But this was no luncheon chime – this was the fire alarm.

A nurse appeared and started to wheel Margaret's bed towards the lifts. Matron followed. As she left the ward, she was sure she spotted flames – a-thunderin' out of control – by the wastepaper basket. It was only a few minutes later, as she hurried out of the building in her wheelchair, that she wondered how the fire had come to start on their floor. Was the Rottington becoming cursed? Or could Agatha Bilke's poltergeist really be causing mayhem?

Once in the car park, the designated emergency meeting point, Matron's mobile phone rang – it was Coddles.

"I hear there's a fire at the hospital," he barked. "This doesn't add up. I'm coming over."

Cakebread wished he would stop meddling. She wanted to solve this mystery on her own.

Over at Police HQ, Coddles slammed the phone down and turned to speak to PC Peas.

"I think we should go undercover so we can blend in. Make some very hush-hush enquiries. You, Peas, will be Staff Nurse Peas. I shall be a humble hospital doctor, who has a PhD in saving the human race from bad stuff. That way no one will know it's us."

26. SAVED

"*Heeeeeeeeeeeeeeeeeeeeeeeeeeeeeelllllllllllllllllllll-llppppppppppppppppppp! Cadavers!*"

Cauliflower Trinkle woke up in the mortuary drawer, screaming. It was a good thing that her voice was so loud because it would save her from an almost certain death. Mr Antipathy the porter opened the drawer and got a big shock.

"Agatha Bilke! You're alive! Blimey!"

*It was a good thing that Cauliflower's voice was so
loud because it would save her from an almost certain death*

27. KERBOOM!

Holbeck's parents had left him at home all night while they attended the *WobblyWubbley 24-Hour Charity Marathon Auction 3000*. Now it was coming to an end they were tired. They hadn't slept at all, so busy were they bidding on items donated by celebrities. Mrs Folbeck had made several purchases including a glass eye and an extremely small carrot, both donated by a TV presenter (she had purposefully forgotten that she had a cash-flow problem). Their own donation, a case of *Deluxe Superbio* Mints, had gone for a record price and they were delighted to have helped make money for a worthy cause. What's more, those famous doctors – Tim and Alan Humphrey – had hosted the whole event.

As they left the venue, Mrs Folbeck switched on her

mobile. Better ring her darling boy and check he was all right.

His phone was off. She tried the mansion – no reply.

"I can't believe this! Where is Vickers?"

"Outrageous! You just can't get the staff!" said her husband.

"Sack the lot of them!"

"Call the police!"

"Organise a manhunt!"

"Led by Kofi Annan!"

As Dr Tim Humphrey left the auction venue with his stage costumes (prawn, town crier, teapot) under his arm, he heard the Folbecks kicking up a stink.

"Can I be of any assistance?" he asked, impressed by the generous amounts they had pledged to the Wobbly Wubbley fundraiser only hours before.

"Oh, it's nothing," said Mrs F. "We just can't locate our son."

"Children, eh?" said Dr Tim, who worked with kids and felt he knew a lot about them.

"If you ever need any help, just come to us."

He handed over a business card, which had details of the *All-New TreadQuietly Clinic for Intriguing Children*.

Kerboooooooooooooooooooooooooooooooooooooooom!

Mr and Mrs Folbeck

Suddenly, there were shards of glass, as big as sabres, flying around. The air was charged with tiny fragments of metal. Everyone ducked for cover as the auction house went up in flames. By the time the ambulances came, most of the ~~geese~~ guests were in a deep state of shock. The Folbecks and the Humphrey Doctors sustained only minor injuries but were rushed to the Rottington anyway.

28. DEATH-TRAP

As hungry flames licked the Rottington building above her, Cauliflower Trinkle felt cold and dazed in the basement. She looked Mr Antipathy in the eye.

"So you're not dead then, Miss Bilke," he said. "Deary me, heads will roll over this one. Heads will roll."

"Where am I? Who are you?"

"You are hospital number 37655901. Agatha Bilke. Heartless ex-patient of Ward Ten. Officially," he lowered his voice, as he was prone to do, "you are dead. A goner. Finito. But we must have got that bit wrong. Mistakes can happen so never mind. Out you hop."

Cauliflower tried to lift herself up but her limbs wouldn't work.

"Better call you a doctor," said the strange porter, who

had not seemed to notice that the fire alarm had sounded a few minutes ago and that a) there were no doctors around and b) he was deep in the bowels of a burning building.

Back up at the main door, Agatha was being faced with a decision. Some might call it life and death. Or death and life (which isn't such a popular expression). She *had* to find Cauliflower to make sure she was all right, but the hospital was going up in flames. Any sensible person would have waited for the emergency services to arrive but Agatha had a newfound conscience. She could not stand by while Cauliflower perished – it was her responsibility to find her safe and well. Since the top part of the Rottington was on fire but not the bottom, Bilke reasoned that she would be perfectly fine nipping down the stairs – never mind that the building might collapse in the next few minutes. She knew the route to the mortuary and slipped past a nurse at the main door.

"But doctor!" cried the nurse – for Agatha was still in her scrubs. "You can't go in there! It's a death-trap!"

The girl raced along the corridor leading to the mortuary. The fire had not yet reached this part of the hospital. All was quiet.

"*Cauliflower!* I'm so sorry!" She exclaimed as she entered the still-cold room. She ran to Trinkle and hugged her.

"What's going on?" said Cauliflower. "This man just called me Agatha and he said I was dead. I don't understand."

"We better get you out of here." The real Agatha looked at Antipathy. "Why are you just standing around? We're in the middle of a raging fire!!"

The porter suddenly came to his senses. "Hang on – we need to get out of here!" Due to his normal circumstances (being surrounded by dead people) he took little heed of things like fire alarms, but today was different. There were three people who all needed to keep breathing.

"Let's go!"

Cauliflower was a little unsteady on her feet so they walked slowly until they got out into the light. They made their way carefully up to the top of the stairs where a doctor with a sore nose met them.

"Aha! Agatha Bilke! I knew you couldn't really be dead. As our number one suspect, I'm arresting you for starting lots of little fires in Rottington and Yeovil Town Hall. I'm also arresting you for destroying a helicopter and embarrassing a police officer."

"But you're a doctor," said Antipathy. "You don't have powers of arrest."

"Yes I do," said Coddles.

"Yes he does," said a man dressed as a nurse who was lurking behind him.

"It's Inspector Coddles in disguise," said Agatha, wearily. "Perhaps we should flee this inferno before he starts enforcing the law."

Kerboooooooooooooooooooooooooooooooooooooooooom!

Large bits of ceiling fell around them. The ground shook. Cauliflower trembled.

"Come on everyone, get out!"

They scrambled out of the building, narrowly escaping a huge ball of flame that had been hurtling towards them. Agatha really thought she'd seen it all – as far as fires were concerned – but this blaze was big, of Hollywood proportions. All the other patients standing outside gazed up in awe as bits of the Rottington fell apart. It was an incredible picture of destruction.

Agatha smiled at Cauliflower. She was unharmed. But wait! Holbeck! She had left him in A&E, which was on the ground floor – and by now there was very little left of the ground floor. She looked around – she couldn't see him anywhere. She had saved Cauliflower only to sacrifice her beloved! ~~Oh, passion. It's a funny thing.~~

"Agatha, I meant what I said just now. I still have to arrest you." Coddles was extremely irritating. He fished out a pair of handcuffs from his pocket and waggled them in front of her. Just as he clipped them round her wrists, a voice could be heard from across the car park:

"A*aaaaa*gatha!"

29. A HUNDRED POLICEMEN

"Why has my sist*aaaa*h been handcuffed?" Margaret was not happy. "She hasn't done *aaaa*nything wrong."

"We've got her! We've got her! We have GOT HER! Ha!" Coddles was jumping up and down.

"Send me one hundred policemen – including police ladies if pertinent," shouted Coddles, becoming somewhat out of breath. "We shall surround her and perhaps shoot a small plastic bullet above her head. Also, we need to get her DNA, Peas."

"Please."

"PEAS! *Frizz!* Just do it."

PC Peas did what he was told and retrieved a small spatula from his pocket, ready to scoop some skin cells from the terrible girl. Meanwhile Coddles read from his notebook:

"Agatha Bilke, where were you on the night of the 25th? And the 26th, 27th, the morning of the 28th, 29th (afternoon and evening), 30th all day and –"

"Coddles, I'm innocent – and I have to find Holbeck!" yelled Agatha. "Get me out of these handcuffs!"

"Well that's what you get for starting a nasty little fire like the one we have here. I saw you racing out of the building just now, didn't I? Caught in the act, some might say."

Slowly, it dawned on Agatha that she really was in a fix. She could not prove that she wasn't in the Rottington when the fire was started. Cauliflower had been locked in a drawer at the time. Holbeck had been unconscious so he could hardly be considered a reliable witness – and besides, he may well have kicked the bucket by now. No one could vouch for her.

"What's going on?" Matron wheeled over.

"Er, Cakebread… I thought you were dead – that I'd killed you…" Agatha was more than a little unnerved.

"We thought *you* were dead," said matron. "They found you in the mortuary so we all had a cry and then someone played the banjo."

"Agatha Bilke, where were you on the night of the 25th? And the 26th, 27th, the morning of the 28th, 29th (afternoon and evening)..."

Despite the pencil in her stomach, the senior nurse seemed rather perky. She spotted Cauliflower: "Hurrah! We have solved the mystery!"

Suddenly, somebody shrieked.

"*Oh no!* It's the girl with no heart! Get her out of here! Get her out! She must be the devil!" Mrs Folbeck appeared from behind a tent. "She mustn't go near my darling boy! He's in that makeshift operating theatre receiving life-saving treatment!"

So Holbeck was not burnt to a crisp! Agatha was so relieved that even the Folbecks' loud complaining didn't annoy her. Dr Tim, who had travelled with them to the hospital, now emerged sipping a cup of tea out of a polystyrene cup. He was delighted when he spotted his old patient.

"Agatha! How are things? It's been months and months! Now, your rehabilitation program?"

"You *know* this monstrosity?!" exclaimed Mrs Folbeck.

"Of course, it's our friend, the renowned arsonist but – hopefully – new-found good egg. You *have* been sticking to your Humphrey Technique, Agatha? You *haven't* let us down, have you?"

Agatha smiled faintly and decided to say nothing. So Holbeck had been pulled from the blaze and was now getting immediate attention. She couldn't discover exactly what was wrong but Dr Alan said it was serious. Meanwhile, Cauliflower was talking to PC Peas, who was showing her a map of the country, with the location of each fire clearly circled in red. Miss Trinkle was shaking her head.

"Coddles! Release my sist*aaaa*h!" blurted Margaret.

But the policeman was adamant and insisted that Agatha accompany him to the station. No one could vouch for her and he would not give in. She needed a miracle.

"My my! It's the surgeon!" said the man from Peerage Avenue. "Saved any more lives then? Are you taking a break from the burns victims?"

Suddenly among them was the only person in the world who had seen Agatha's good side (even if she had lurched about a bit while driving). He was her alibi.

"I have just had some wonderful news! I don't have a brain tumour, as the medics thought!" He was in the most joyous of moods. "And this young doctor," he patted Agatha on the back, "gave me an interesting lift to hospital – perhaps the best journey of my life! She was helping a very sick boy from Peerage Avenue to A&E. She's all heart, this surgeon. All heart. But you can imagine my surprise when I got here and the place was on fire. They gave me my prognosis by the bins."

The gathered crowd were agog. Could this jolly man really be describing Agatha Bilke? The worst person in the country? Surely not.

The man gave her a £50 note.

"Buy something nice for yourself."

"See," said Margaret – who would *never* discover who ran her over – pinching Peas's arm. "A*aaa*gatha *didn't* start *aaa*ll those fires."

"You can't give that Beelzebub money!" Mrs Folbeck rushed forward, ripping the cash from Agatha's hand. "Give *us* the cash – it's compensation. If Agatha was in Peerage Avenue, she must have been with our son! Put the girl in jail and throw away the key!"

Agatha glanced at the nasty parents and thought of their despotic map of Britain, invading the privacy of every mint-lover in Britain. They didn't *really* care about their son. They cared only about themselves, their status and wealth. Agatha suddenly felt sorry for Holbeck. The privilege he was born to was meaningless.

Coddles reluctantly unlocked the handcuffs and with that Agatha was free.

30. RED SPOTS

Lynda and Dennis rushed over to Agatha.

"Agatha!" Lynda raced to hug her. "You're back! Did you go anywhere nice? Can I come too next time? We were due to be chucked out of here today. They probably had to start that big fire to get us to leave because we had a sit-in. It was everso good. We had placards and everything."

In addition, both children had painted large red spots on their faces and hands, as if to suggest new diseases. But Agatha noticed that Lynda was without her drip.

"I think I've grown out of it," said Peanuts. "It was a bit boring, wheeling it around everywhere.

"We heard about your X-ray," she continued. "And we think it's really cool."

Lynda winked, then spotted her mum and ran to her.

Agatha found herself alone. She wasn't off the hook yet. After all she *had* had something to do with the helicopter crash. And it didn't help that everyone seemed to have seen the X-ray. Lynda knew, as did Dennis, matron, the Folbecks, the police... and so, presumably, did the entire nursing staff and the rest of the patients at the Rottington. She felt in her pocket. She still had the keys to the ambulance, she could drive off quickly... but presumably they would have the number plate logged by now. The best thing to do would be to walk.

Agatha gazed at the Rottington, blazing above. Everyone had escaped ~~I'd like some biscuits now~~ unscathed and the fire was almost under control now. But the flames did not excite her as they billowed from the windows. There was a time when she would have congratulated herself on such chaos. Although she hadn't started the Rottington fire, it would have been the icing on the cake after a series of wonderful, dangerous events. She had even risen from the dead for heaven's sake. But Agatha was not proud – she was preoccupied.

Agatha peered round the tent to check on Holbeck. He was surrounded by surgeons – she couldn't see him. How would she let him know where she'd gone? Perhaps they did have a future together. Away from his parents, he might become the Holbeck she knew in the Rottington. She asked Dr Tim for a piece of paper and a pen, quickly scribbled a note and gave it to Tim to give it to the boy when he was better. She knew she could trust the doctor.

By now, all sorts of patients were complaining about charred underclothes, the lack of catering and needing their medication. Cauliflower was still trying to convince Peas that she knew nothing (about any explosions).

No one would notice if Agatha sloped off. Here was her chance. As she started to wander in the direction of the park where she had first seen Coddles' helicopter, she hoped Holbeck would find her at some point. Agatha walked away – like she always did.

Back inside the hospital, Agatha's X-ray bubbled and popped in the heat on the mortuary floor, where the fire had finally spread. It was quite difficult to see now, but if you were to look very very closely, you would notice that there was a small speck where the heart should be.

31. NEVER TRUST A MICRO CHIP

Superintendent Peas handed the report to his deputy. Coddles could not believe it. So the random fires had been started by a rogue micro chips inserted into packets of mints. Ridiculous.

"Why on earth would someone do that?"

Peas raised his eyebrows as if to suggest that people were quite mad. As he did so, his stomach rumbled and he realised he had not had any breakfast this morning.

"The Folbecks wanted to monitor every packet of mints sold," he said. "But the technology was primitive and the chips were faulty. The packets had a tendency to spontaneously combust at any time, thus causing these mysterious – but now not-so-mysterious – fires. It wasn't Agatha Bilke who set the hospital alight at all; it was

Cakebread who left an empty packet of *Deluxe Superbios* in the ward. All the other fires were started by unsuspecting mint-chewers."

"Can we arrest her?"

"I don't think so."

Coddles was annoyed. Agatha Bilke had slipped through his grasp again – she had disappeared in an instant. He tried to think laterally... perhaps Agatha had logged on to an Internet chat-room... Something like the forum at Fieryfire.com. He could find her and regain his ~~digestives, please~~ credibility. Must get her for that helicopter crash, he thought, the case was, after all, still open.

The Folbecks had been prosecuted under the Invasion of Privacy laws. *No one* was allowed to see where and when people were eating mints. With his parents now broke, Holbeck had been sent to a nice comprehensive school. His leg had cleared up, but he now had trouble sleeping. Mummy would buy him herbal remedies but they didn't really work. (They let out the east wing of the mansion to someone off the telly.) Holbeck vowed to find Agatha one day; he would never forget her.

Matron's love of washing machines had temporarily subsided but in its place was an interest in the climate of Helsinki. However, she soon suffered further stomach pains and had to have the pencil removed. Of course, she wondered how on earth it had got in there, but she framed it and hung it on her wall as a nice memento anyway.

Epilogue – Rottington Syndrome

There was still one patient left in Ward Ten. Cauliflower needed specialist help for her particular ailment.

The doctors Humphrey were brought in to help. With their treatment, it was hoped, Cauliflower would learn what it was like to be inside her own head.

They built a set in the newly refurbished basement of the Rottington and, when she got down there, Cauliflower was confronted by what looked like an adventure plaground. There was a mass of brightly coloured tubes covered by large sections of pink polystyrene. There were balls suspended inside the tubes, there was a large round thing that looked like a head with a sign pointing to it that read: BRAINUS PROBLEMUS. Money had clearly been spent; the maze was the size of a large passenger aircraft.

"Hullo!" called Tim from behind a tube. He emerged with a spanner in his hand and a clipboard in the other.

"Just been making last minute adjustments! So... Cauldron, what's the problem?"

"It's Cauliflower."

"What? You're frightened of cauliflowers? Oh dear — well, I'm sure we can customise this thing somehow."

"No, my name's Cauliflower. And I like Cauliflowers, actually."

"What about other foods? Scared of grapes?"

"No."

"Er, bit iffy on the subject of tangerines?"

Cauliflower looked blank.

"Leopards? Pavements? Dental floss?"

"It's just the shouting."

Cauliflower often wondered how her dear friend Agatha was — and whether she would ever get back in touch. She still had peculiar visions of an operating theatre but she did not know where these hallucinations came from — or when they had first appeared. Perhaps they would never leave her.

"Yelps! Causes drowsiness!!" She blurted at Tim; she couldn't help herself.

"Ah yes, the exclamations. Hm. *Rottington Syndrome* we can call it. We'll *definitely* be able to help you, young lady."

He reached into his pocket and handed her a sweet. As he did so, a small note addressed to "Holby" fluttered out onto the floor.

"Would you like a mint? I found a packet down the back of a cupboard."

Dr Tim tossed the empty packet away. It was not long before it started smouldering in the corner.

Siân Pattenden has been a journalist for a few years, working for titles including *Smash Hits*, *NME*, *The Face* and the *Guardian*. She has also been on the telly and radio. She is married to songwriter Luke Haines and has a son called Fred. They live in London. Her first book, *The Awful Tale of Agatha Bilke,* published in 2006, has been short-listed for the Glen Dimplex Award, the Sheffield Children's Book Award and the Branford Boase Award.